A. Cazenave, Ernest Feydeau

Female Beauty

The art of human decoration

A. Cazenave, Ernest Feydeau

Female Beauty
The art of human decoration

ISBN/EAN: 9783337370763

Printed in Europe, USA, Canada, Australia, Japan

Cover: Foto ©Andreas Hilbeck / pixelio.de

More available books at **www.hansebooks.com**

FEMALE BEAUTY;

OR,

THE ART OF HUMAN DECORATION.

BY DR. A. CAZENAVE.

AND

THE ART OF PLEASING:

BY ERNEST FEYDEAU.

Translated from the Original French,
BY MISS M. T. NASH.

" Le beau s'adresse a l'âme,
Le joli s'adresse au goût."

NEW YORK:
G. W. Carleton & Co., Publishers.
PARIS: DENTU.
M.DCCC.LXXIV.

Maclauchlan, Printer and Stereotyper,
56, 58 & 60 Park St., N. Y.

CONTENTS.

——:o:——

PREFACE.

BEAUTY has at all times been a theme of song for poets. It has always been the object of passionate adoration by artists; while observers, philosophers, and scholars have also, in all ages, made it the subject of serious study. Men eminent by their merit have given this question a large place in their writings; and they did not confine themselves to defining that quality as one of the most precious gifts that Heaven has given to mankind, but they often investigated what means would best preserve corporal beauty and render it complete, and in some cases supply its deficiency. Go as far

as you may in history, and one finds traces
of the cultivation of beauty—a species of al-
chemic cosmetic which has rendered a multitude of adepts very celebrated. Mythology
tells of Circe, daughter of the Sun, so skilful
in the art of modifying the human exterior
by her artifices, that she passed for an enchantress ; of Medea, who had such marvellous secrets for re-establishing a resemblance
to beauty, that one can say of her, she re-
juvenated the father of Jason. The heroic
times furnish us other celebrated names in
that art, which, twenty centuries ago, they
had already pushed to the most exaggerated
limits of refinement. These names belong
mostly to the women who played so brilliant a
rôle in the old societies of Greece and Rome.
We cite Aspasia, one of the most charming
models of Attic grace. This beautiful Phor-
cienne has united in a book, cited by Aétius,
a certain number of prescriptions, dedicated
to women who were anxious to augment and
preserve their beauty, some of which are in-
spired by an exact knowledge of hygiene,
and merit to be preserved by tradition. They

refer especially to the use of baths, lotions, a choice of clothing, and certain habits of domestic life. After "Aspasia," one must cite Cleopatra, to whom is attributed a little work dedicated to women, containing a large number of recipes for cosmetics. The fathers of medicine did not disdain to give a place in their writings to this science, so often dishonored by quacks. Here and there are noticed the curious ideas of Moschion, Heraclitus of Tarentum, Aétius, and Galen. The question was often discussed if the art of preserving beauty was essentially and exclusively the domain of quackery; or if, on the contrary, it touched medicine in certain limits, or even took an important place in it. Doubt is impossible on this point, if one consults very serious authorities, who have declared its rationality and scientific value, which may be called the treatment of beauty. Without doubt, a great number of works written on this subject have only occasioned the employment of useless, if not dangerous, drugs. This circumstance is to be regretted. The desire to renew faded charms, or hide

1*

the elements of natural ugliness, is as old
as the civilized world, and has at all times
provoked quackery. Is it not astonishing,
in spite of the blame men animated by
the love of morality and humanity have
laid against it, that its excessive use con-
tinues and prevails to the present day? The
fathers of the church have said all in their
power against the use of artifices for the
toilette, which women use with a veritable
passion. Tertullian treated those practices
as diabolical by which so many matrons
were so skilful in coloring their lips, whitening their skin, and animating the brilliancy
of their eyes by blackening the lids. The
same passion is found in "Rules for Young
Ladies," by Cyprian and Basil Le Grand,
but above all in the teaching of Clement
of Alexandria, where one may read the excessive use of cosmetics, and if one reflects
on the composition of most of the lotions
and pomades prepared for the toilette, they
would understand how just are the protesta-
tions contained in his work. However, it
would be almost impossible to enumerate all

the strange compositions found in drugs more or less unhealthy, and reproduced for centuries. It is from that inexhaustible source is taken at all times so much unrestrained quackery; but it is there also that is found the cause of so much renown attributed to the most of these productions, not to speak of the difficulties belonging to their employ, and the complicated composition that appears really monstrous. But, in spite of all these causes, it is not to be doubted that the art of cosmetics is important as regards health. In fact, true beauty cannot exist without health; if health fails, beauty fades. There is then occasion for serious medical treatment. Among the specialists who have occupied themselves with the embellishments of the human body, first to be cited is Mercuriali, who wrote a very serious, remarkably able, and original work. It is evident that this work served as a model for others written during his time, such as those of Villeneuf, Fioramenti, Argelata, etc. This new work on "Human Decoration" is destined to supply an important blank in a science re-

plete with interest, wants, and legitimate de-
sires. It is written in a simple, methodical
form, easy to consult, placing within reach
of everybody the means of beautifying the
human form. Only such rules are given
which long experience and complete knowledge have shown to be useful ; and authors
who have written the most complete works on
human embellishment have followed nearly
the same plan, studying, one by one, all
parts of the human body, commencing with
the head, the principal seat of beauty. After
general considerations on beauty, our series
of remarks on embellishment will commence
with the head, examining its different parts
thus : the complexion, hair, forehead, ears,
eyes, nose, mouth, and chin. We will then
study the trunk, which comprises the neck,
shoulders, chest, armpits, back, waist, etc.
The members that come after, are the arms,
wrists, hands, nails, thighs, legs, feet, and
toes. We propose to explain in a special
chapter the embellishment of the skin in
general ; natural exhalations, corpulence,
thinness, and the means of remedying them,

combined with a few remarks on cosmetics, perfumes, etc. Ancient prescriptions merit a general reproach, for sinning by the multiplicity of their recipes and affectation. To resume, "human decoration" is the domain of medical practice and family habits. It is addressed at the same time to physicians and people of the world. In this work, the resources are indicated for embellishing every part of the body, in the most simple and agreeable form possible, without trouble, and especially without danger to the health. Its object is intended to meet the requirements of all natural wants and necessities. We hope that this book will merit the confidence and gratitude of all persons for whom it is designed, without losing in the eyes of any one the object of an earnest work.

PERSONAL BEAUTY.

CHAPTER I.

BEAUTY IN GENERAL:

ITS MEANING, ITS DIFFERENCE AND VALUE.

FEMALE BEAUTY.

OCRATES called it a short tyranny; Plato, the privilege of Nature. Absolute beauty, which appears possible to define, has been the object of a certain number of prescriptions, which render more or less agreeable the idea attached to it. Plato considered beauty the harmony of the soul with the mind; Aristotle, as united to a certain grandeur, abstract and ideal. Galilian, considering it more explicit and more material, sought beauty in a conformity of members, high colors, soft flesh, a certain elasticity of form, and harmony of traits. The most eminent philosophers have tried to bring formulas for physical beauty to exact rules. Among modern authors who occupy themselves with this arduous matter, one finds very explicit formulas. Thus Albert Dürer and Mercuriali—one an artist, the other a physician—considered a good disposition resulting from a perfect constitution as beauty. Fallope pressed the question closer; for him, beauty was a natural state of the body, a habitude consistent in the harmony of substance, disposition, form, and color. The sentiment of beauty varies according to taste and prejudice. The Orientals, among whom idleness is an honor, think a fleshy woman the highest type of female beauty; while Occidental nations generally prefer slightness of form, and grace of expression. Beauty varies according to age and sex. In youth it reveals a particular freshness, ingenuousness, and gentleness, not to be found in adult age. Here beauty has attractions that speak above all to the senses. In old age, on the contrary, it addresses itself to the mind, by its air of gravity and dignity.

"Vermilion lips, well shaped, a smiling mouth, beautiful white teeth, an elastic step, plump cheeks, charm at eighteen," said the philosopher Diderot. "To-day it is a timid young girl walking in silence with her mother, that attracts and charms me. Who has the best taste? Is it I at eighteen? Is it I at fifty? Fine question! At eighteen it is not the image of beauty, but the physiognomy of pleasure, which attracts me."

Manly beauty consists in dignity of character, force, and pride, the traits firm and decided. In woman it is principally grace that predominates: her form is finer and more delicate; her traits are distinguished by harmony of the lineaments, her form by its grace. Philosophers sought to establish a correlative between the corporal constitution of both sexes, and said woman's body is more rounded, more flexible, and smoother

than man's ; her muscles are less apparent,
more delicate, and more supple. Her sentiments are finer, and her sensibility keener.
Man is just the contrary. In a moral sense,
he is grave, resolute, and tenacious ; bears
bodily fatigue much easier than woman.
Beauty varies according to the time, the
people, the taste, and prejudices. Yet the
most eloquent tongues have failed to find an
exact definition of this most charming attri-
bute of human nature. To find a formula
that will satisfy all opinions, it should be
composed of all instincts, sentiments, passions, that give birth to the cultivation of
beauty. That is simply impossible ; beauty,
from a general point of view, is a harmonious *ensemble.* The principal elements that
serve to form it all are : a just proportion of
all the members, transparency of the skin,
and freshness of color. These qualities only
make a beautiful statue. To find the celes-
tial fire that animates it, must be added the
expression of sentiments reflected from the
soul beaming in the look, the smile, the
actions, and even the accent. But what ·

characterizes beauty above *all*, and gives it irresistible power, is grace ; with its indefinite charm it is nothing, yet it *is all*. Beauty is the flower, and grace the perfume. The question of beauty was pushed so far, that Xenophore said that the possession of beauty was above that of science, fortune, virtue, and all the advantages with which mankind could be favored. This is an exaggeration that we will leave entirely to poets and artists ; but for philosophers and serious observers, it is none the less true, that beauty is one of the most beautiful gifts that Heaven has given mankind. Without doubt the qualities of the heart and mind have an incontestable excellence ; but in point of view of human perfection, their value is incomplete without beauty. On the contrary, nothing more perfect can be imagined, nor give a better idea of the divine essence of man, than beauty of body united to goodness of heart, elevation of mind, and purity of soul.

If, in mythology, Juno, Venus, and Minerva disputed, it was not for a question of

power, but a question of charms. All the
great heroes were types of superhuman
beauty. Homer used all the resources of
his epic muse to paint Hector and Achilles
with almost divine charms. Antiquity rep-
resents the Indian Bacchus as a type. History informs us that Achideanus, king of
Lacedæmonia, was condemned by his people
to a heavy fine for having married a little
ugly woman, who could not bear fine children. They wanted great, handsome men
to sustain and command the republics and
empires.

But apart from these examples, the
influence of beauty is seen and felt everywhere. In woman above all, it has the
power of exercising an influence over those
that come in contact with it, and is for
her the most precious of all gifts, for it
gives her a moral force that defies all
physical weakness. We may say it per-
suades better than eloquence, and shares
with morality the power of inspiring sentiment. It is then principally to woman we
address our counsels. Our task is great, for

we have not only to tell her how to preserve her beauty, but inform those to whom nature has refused, or illness deprived of, their charms, the means of supplying them. To arrive surely at this end, we must impress this first truth : that the foundation of corporal beauty is health.

In effect, take the latter, and the former alters, fades, and disappears. The duty of the physician is then to seek to re-establish the pathological state, which is so often for beauty a source of obliteration and ruin.

Particular care follows—which is of great importance in a double point of view—as to what must be done, and what must be left undone.

Under this heading, I propose to study preservation and embellishment of the body in all points that touch beauty, especially those parts that are constantly exposed to view, and require the most particular care.

THE FACE.

All harmonious expressions are united in the human figure.—ST. PIERRE.

"A beautiful face is the finest of all spectacles."

THE head is particularly the seat of beauty. On the face dwells I know not what, that charms and attracts us. We admire a pretty foot, are struck by an elegant waist: a well-made arm, a pretty hand, captivates our attention; but we are never so strongly attracted by any part of the body as by the face. All other organs bear a general resemblance, but in the face there is a vast difference; each countenance has its particular type of beauty.

The face is the seat of that inexplicable expression that draws heart to heart and soul to soul. Liebaut said: "We kiss the hand of the woman we love with respect, but it is always with a sentiment of affection that we kiss the face."

True beauty in general does not result from the perfect form of one or two members, but in the harmony of all. It is the air and physiognomy that attract or repulse us. For those who read the face it may well be called the mirror that reflects the purity of soul, the elevation of the mind, goodness of heart, all charms, modesty, pride, benevolence, friendship ; but above all, love—true love—is written in the traits of the physiognomy.

Lavater cites a passage from "Clarissa Harlowe" on the remarkable *finesse* of Miss Howe on the physiognomies that Solmes, Hickmann, and Lovelace must have had at college. "I'll tell you the lights in which Hickmann, Solmes, and Lovelace, our three heroes, have appeared to me, supposing them boys at school. Solmes I have imagined to be a little sordid, pilfering rogue, who would purloin from everybody and beg everybody's bread and butter from him, while, as I have heard a reptile brag, he would on a winter's morning spit upon his thumbs and spread his own with it, that he might keep it all to himself. Hickmann, a great overgrown, lank-haired, chubby boy, who would be hunched and punched by everybody, and go home with his fingers in his eye and tell his mother. While Lovelace I have supposed a curly-pated villain, full of fire, fancy, and mischief; an orchard robber, a wall-climber, a horse-rider, without saddle or bridle, neck or nothing; a sturdy rogue in short, who would kick and cuff, and do no right and take no wrong of anybody; would get his head broke, then a plaster for it, or let it heal of itself, while he went on to do more mischief, and if not to get, to deserve, broken bones."

And the same dispositions have grown up with them and distinguished them as men, with no natural alteration.

THE COMPLEXION.

La beauté la plus régulière ne saurait me séduire, si la fraîcheur, la pureté, l'éclat de son teint, ne s'animent d'un rayon de jeunesse et de santé.—L. CAMUS.

HE most perfect beauty is unattractive when freshness and health are gone· Several circumstances unite to give great value to the physiognomy. One of the first conditions of beauty of face is beauty of complexion.

Diderot, the philosopher, said, "I have seen in the Faubourg children the most charming faces at twelve and thirteen years of age : eyes full of gentleness, intrepid and ardent, the neck round and full of muscles, the cheeks plump ; yet at times I have seen the pretty mouth strangely altered, the neck covered with wrinkles, and the whole physiognomy changed, either from exposure, anger, or other causes. One cannot begin too early the education of children. I have known families in which one word of command was severely followed: there was

2

never any anger, never a loud word pronounced, before the children."

There is always a certain amount of delicacy, more or less great, according to the individual, and there are certain thick skins, on which the emotions of the soul reflect themselves in an unappreciable manner to the sight.

A beautiful complexion is agreeable when the colors of the skin, white, vermilion, pure, tender, and polished, are accessible to the modifications produced by the impressions of the soul, without being easily altered by emotion.

This delicacy of complexion belongs exclusively to women.

One of the best means to preserve beauty of tint is to avoid as much as possible all occasions which sooner or later trouble the mind ; to accustom one's self early to resist demonstrative emotions, either of great joy or sorrow.

Generally speaking, cold air is a mortal enemy of the complexion : nevertheless there are exceptions with persons of high color, who support it easily; while those of a pale tint find themselves better in warm air.

The manner of living in point of view of alimentation has a great influence on the complexion, because there is an intimate relation between the state of the stomach and the tint of the complexion. Persons of high color spoil their complexion by using irritating aliments.

Others fall into the excess of eating insufficient, hoping to preserve freshness of complexion; they only injure their stomach, and give themselves a pale, bluish tint.

Even tight clothes have an important influence on the complexion. From what I have said, it will be easily understood that in the observance of hygienic rules will be found the best means of preserving the delicacy and purity of the complexion.

It is well not to give the stomach all it craves. Persons subject to a rush of blood to the head should eat plain food and avoid all stimulating drinks, such as pure wines, liquors, etc. For those of a pale complexion it is quite the contrary.

Many are in the habit of taking something strengthening in the morning, and sleep afterwards.   This is wrong.   A glass of cold water taken on rising and fast an hour after, is very good.

Many take injections to preserve freshness of complexion.   It is an evident exaggeration, but quite harmless when not abused.

As to the general rules of hygiene, they are applicable here.   To sleep too much is as bad as not to sleep enough.   A too active life has as many disadvantages as a too inactive one.

We have seen frequent alterations produced by tan and sunburn.   Various means are proposed as protection against them, among' which are a number of lotions and pomades.

A veil is an excellent article.   That which I prefer most is a little pure rice powder or pulverized starch, or one of the following mixtures :

Starch........................	1 pound.
Sub-nitrate of Bismuth.............	3 ounces.

ROSE POWDER.

Rice Powder......................	2 pounds.
Lake Carmine......................	4 drachms.
Essence of Rose....................	18 grains.
Essence of Santal..................	18 grains.

Mix well.

Spread it on the face with a hare's foot, or, better still, a tuft of down.

The simplest protection for the face from cold air is a veil. Avoid sitting too close to the fire or in the sun.

Wet the face as little as possible. Lotions should never be hot nor cold ; tepid are best. There are certain skins that can only be cleaned with powder.

How many women have preserved a fresh, delicate, transparent complexion, who scarcely ever wet it !

I shall say the same of greasy substances, pomades, etc. We shall see later they are only to be used in exceptional cases. For still stronger reasons every kind of paint should be avoided. La Bruyère says : "If women wish to appear beautiful only in their own eyes, they may follow their own taste in

ornament;" but if they wish to please the
men, he declares that red and white make
them hideous.

Now, if we seek means to remedy the
alteration of the complexion, we shall find
much greater difficulties, because it is subject to very different *inquiries;* consequently
needs different means to remedy it.

We have already spoken of the aid which
health naturally furnishes to those who desire purity of complexion.

I will not return again to the value of
general means. I cannot, however, resist
declaring that two therapeutic agents quite *à
la mode* are enemies of the complexion. I
allude to sea-bathing and iron. I do not con-
clude that one should never have recourse to
them, nor should sacrifice however little of the
health for beauty; but I am influenced by a
long experience not to advise the indifferent
use of these methods of restoration, and especially not to abuse them, as is often the case.

As to local means, they·are naturally very
different and variable, according to the constitution and alteration of the skin.

The following formulas may be used :

Bichloride Hydrargyria................ 2 grains.
Chlorhydrate Ammonia................ 2 grains.
Milk of Almonds..................... ½ pint.

This is one of the best cosmetics for the complexion, especially for fine, delicate skins, that are sometimes slightly farinaceous, and cannot bear any kind of greasy substance.

This liquid is employed in a pure state, with a fine linen rag. If necessary, it may be mixed with an equal portion of water ; that is, should it prove irritating for an excessively delicate skin. In any case, it should be used with great care.

Chlorate of Potash.................. 18 grains.
Glycerine......................... 1 ounce.
Rose-water......................... ½ pint.
    Mix carefully for lotions.

For those whose skin is greasy and inclined to pimples—

Bicarbonate of Soda................ 18 grains.
Distilled Water...................... ½ pint.
Essence of Portugal................ 6 drops.

The face may also be washed with elder water, weak tea, distilled linden water, milk of almonds, virginal milk.

Virginal Milk.....................
Rose-water........ .... 1 pint.
Tincture of Benzoin.... .... 1 drachm.
  Mix the water slowly with the tincture.

In general, lotions for the face should be made of a mild temperature. A lotion too cold is as prejudicial to the complexion as one too warm.

It is better to mix them in the evening, scarcely drying the face when applied. In the morning wipe gently with a linen rag dipped in pure water and cologne.

When the skin is dry, rough, and one wishes to efface spots, pomades are recommended, either of cold cream or cucumber.

The following are excellent :

POMADE FOR THE COMPLEXION.

Oil of Bitter Almonds................ .... 1 scruple.
Spermaceti............... 1 drachm, 2 scruples.
Galien Cerate .... 1 ounce.

POMADE.

Oil of Bitter Almonds	1 drachm.
Fresh Butter	4 drachms.
Lard	4 drachms.
Mutton Suet	2 drachms.

Wash in rose-water, and add wax, sufficient quantity.

POMADE FOR PIMPLES.

Bicarbonate of Soda	2 scruples.
Glycerine	1 drachm.
Spermaceti Pomade	1 ounce.

Mix.

POMADE FOR GREASY COMPLEXION.

Acetate of Zinc	2 grains.
Cold Cream	1 ounce.
Essence of Roses	10 drops.

Lotions like pomades should be employed at night, and always moderately. Lotions may be employed in the morning, especially if a pomade has been used the night previous.

Another means of preserving freshness of complexion is the use of pastes, applied to the face in the form of a mask during the night, and is taken off in the morning with a little cervil water.

2*

MASK FOR THE FACE.

Barley Flour, sifted.....................	3 ounces.
Honey...........................	1 ounce, 1 scruple.
White of Egg.........................	1 scruple.

Mix as a paste.

ANOTHER.

White Wax	1 ounce.
Sweet Almond Oil.....................	2 ounces.
Goat's Grease.......................	1 ounce.
Powdered Starch.....................	2 scruples.

Make a pomade and anoint the face at night.

THE HAIR.

THE ancients, who were passionate lovers of beautiful forms, attached great importance to the hair; for it held in itself a question of beauty, and was for them the source and occasion of a great number of ingenious myths, which pleased them much. To-day there is no one who does not feel that the form and color of the hair gives various expressions to the face.

If we cite here and there examples of disdain for the care of the hair (the Hibernians let their hair grow, and used it to wipe their hands when soiled by ignoble repasts), in general we find everywhere the same love, the same culture of it, often exaggerated. Women, especially, have at all times attached an idea of beauty to the hair, which is betrayed by all the refinements of luxury and toilette. Guyon, speaking of corporal beauty, says of the hair: "On the front it should be crimped and curled, and of medium length for men ; for women, long, thick, of a golden color, wavy and glistening." A woman's hair is beautiful when long and abundant, and falls in soft, silky tresses. Certain colors are more or less preferred. To-day we do not think of the goddess of beauty, except with hair falling in heavy masses to her feet.

Natural curls have all the charms for us which the ancients accorded to them. Only the artists of the middle ages, deluded by enthusiasm for a severe creed, imagine for their types of seraphic beauty, stiff, smooth hair framing the face, and not a single wave to relieved its immovable sanctimoniousness.

As to the most beautiful color of the hair, it is now a point very much contested, and it would be very bold to pretend to establish the superiority of one shade above another. It was not the same in ancient times, and if one listens to tradition, which is rarely wrong, it is permissible to believe that golden blonde was in those times what might be called the privileged color.

The most beautiful ancient types, Achilles, Menelaus, Meleager, were blondes. Bacchus, the ideal of ancient beauty, had golden hair. The handsome Narcissus, the favorite of Apollo, was a pale, melancholy blonde. Orpheus, in the picture which he paints of Circe, the redoubtable enchantress, represented her with hair as ardent as the rays of the sun. Catullus sang of the golden locks of Berenice.

The fair Phœbus is a type become commonplace. At Rome, golden hair was particularly in favor. Messalina hid her beautiful black hair under a yellow wig.

"Nigrum flavo crinem abscondente galero."—JUVENAL.

There were, nevertheless, certain exceptions
to this taste of the ancients. The Egyptians,
and generally the Arabs, affected a great
disdain for blonde hair. Apulus praises in
the beautiful Photes her hair black as ebony.
Horace celebrated Lycidas with black hair
and eyes. Solomon, the wisest of kings, and
grand amateur of beauty, praises in his well-
beloved her locks black and brilliant as a
raven's wing. Descending to our own times,
we see that in part, perhaps the epoch in
which we live, the red blonde, so dear to the
ancients, has retained the artistic and poet-
ical value with which it was then surrounded.

Whatever it may be, having been an au-
rora for infancy, the hair adds to the dignity
and majesty of mankind. It relieves and sur-
rounds happily all that there is attractive
and beautiful in a female face ; even for old
age, it is one of the most forcible reasons for
respect. Therefore one can understand the
interest and importance of keeping it in a
healthy condition.

The head becomes gray and bald at an

early age on account of trouble, excessive labor, and late hours; sudden fright, violent grief, and moral emotions. Adrian cites the fact that during the reign of Louis XVI., a gentleman of the court was surprised in the garden with the maid of honor, and being condemned to death for it, was so struck by the terrible sentence, that his hair became white during the night. A similar phenomenon is that of St. Valier, who became suddenly gray on learning that his daughter, Diana de Poitiers, had become the mistress of the king.

The hair becomes white and falls, if the constitution is deteriorated by suffering, privation, imprisonment, or living in a dark and damp atmosphere. To avoid sorrow and grief, is not in the power of all; nevertheless, to a certain extent, we should not allow our sorrow to weigh us down too heavily.

Many ladies are in the habit of doing their hair up very tight; it is a bad habit, because it fatigues the scalp and injures the bulb. Crimping, curling, and braiding the hair have the effect of weakening the roots.

Never use a hot iron. It dries the scalp, burns the skin, breaks the hair, and alters its electric functions. Simplicity is the most becoming ornament for the hair. The coiffure most becoming to women is to wear the hair slightly frizzed and arranged in bands, in such a manner as to permit the air to penetrate.

Loosen it night and morning, brush it with care and roll it loosely. If obliged to draw or knot it tightly, take care to leave it loose a few moments night and morning.

Among the exigencies of the toilet are cosmetics, whose use is often fruitless and sometimes dangerous, on account of their composition, and especially their untimely application.

I have seen many persons who have preserved an abundant head of hair for years, without use of anything but brush and comb. There are, however, many who, be it fancy, custom, or desire to preserve the hair, have recourse to different compositions, which they use indiscriminately, and by a bad choice excite that which they wish to avoid.

Thus with some the hair is habitually dry, and the absence or the diminution of the secretion designed to moisten it, causes it to lose its natural brilliancy, and break easily. If (as occurs too often) one is in the habit of wetting the hair to render it soft and fresh for a time, it makes it still drier, more liable to break and fall off.

In general it is a bad habit to dip the head in cold water morning or night. This remark is more applicable to men than to women. It causes baldness.

Before leaving this subject, I will add that cold baths, and particularly sea-bathing, are enemies of the hair. Some people not only lose their hair, but break and tangle it very easily.

The best and most simple formula is the following :

```
Beef Marrow, prepared................. 1 ounce.
Bitter Almond Oil..................... 2 drachms.
    Mix.
```

Take care to anoint the hair at the roots.

I also cite another, that experience bids me recommend:

Beef Marrow	2 ounces.
Almond Oil	1¼ ounce.
Essence of Lemon	1 drachm.

ANOTHER.

Oil of Roses	2 ounces.
Oil of Vanilla	1 ounce.
Oil of Jessamine	2 drachms.
Oil of Tuberoses	2 drachms.
Oil of Orange Flower	2 drachms.
Essence of Almonds	1 drop.

This oil, besides cleaning the hair, renders it soft and brilliant.

An abundant secretion leaves dandruff on the scalp, which the use of cosmetics only increases. For those whose hair is naturally oily, they should abstain from all kinds of pomades and oils. Brush it carefully night and morning, and use a wash.

The following lotions are excellent:

Water	½ pint.
Carbonate of Soda	1 drachm.
Dissolve, and add the yolks of two eggs well beaten.	

ANOTHER.

Chlorate of Potash	2 scruples.
Rose-water	½ pint.

Dissolve.

ANOTHER.

Borate of Soda	2 scruples.
Distilled Water	½ pint.
Essence of Portugal	18 grains.

ANOTHER.

Ammonia Liquid	18 grains.
Rose-water	½ pint.

To be used in the morning.

OIL FOR THE HAIR.

Oil à la Rose	2 ounces.
Oil à la Vanilla	1 ounce.
Oil à la Jessamine	2 drachms.
Oil à la Tuberose	2 drachms.
Oil à la Orange Flower	2 drachms.
Essence of Almonds	1 drop.
Essence of Cloves	1 drop.

This oil is excellent; besides cleansing, it gives a beautiful lustre.

It is not necessary to advise those who wish to preserve their hair, to avoid all the common preparations that flood the country. There is nothing easier than to preserve the hair, if one will take pains and comb it regularly. Hygienic practice consists in using a fine-tooth comb, separating the hair, and carefully brushing it with a hard brush, so as to excite the bulbs. This should be done particularly on retiring.

Liquid of ammonia and rose-water is an excellent lotion in the morning. This, as well as other prescriptions, should only be used when absolutely necessary, and in any case moderately employed.

For keeping the head clean and preserving the hair, a good stiff brush and comb are the simplest means. An excellent thing for the growth of the hair is to cut the ends from time to time. Mothers often cut the hair of their daughters in second youth, fearing that it may not grow so abundantly if cut when younger. This is an error. The most beauful hair I have ever seen was never touched by the scissors.

The Greeks and Romans had great admiration for the hair of their children ; they regarded it as a robe of innocence.

When full-grown men cut their hair, a

solemn ceremony took place among them. Until then (the poet said) "they would have dishonored the spring-time of their lives." What I have just said is applicable to such mothers who sacrifice the hair of their daughters, and cut it because of its slow growth. Some even shave the hair, be it from sickness or other causes. I do not approve of this. It may be useful from time to time when the hair is too abundant, begins to fall, and fatigues the child. In any case shaving is better than cutting. It often occurs under the influence of age, men particularly become bald; but it should not commence before the fiftieth year of life. Some are prematurely so, be it from excess of grief, labor, or hereditary. It is generally incurable, notwithstanding there are innumerable compositions, all infallible in name. Nevertheless a great number may be tried without disadvantage. Bear's grease was recommended by Cleopatra, to make the hair grow; but I should never finish if I were to give here a complete list of the curious preparations invented for its growth.

I will content myself with citing a few that may be used with a good result.

Beef Marrow........................	1 ounce.
Aromatic Tincture...................	1 drachm.
Mix.	

For washing the head, dip a little linen cloth in the following liquids :

Tincture of Sulphate of Quinine....	
Aromatic Tincture...............	} *equal parts.*
Mix.	

Ammonia Liquid.....................	1 drachm.
Essence of Bitter Almonds.............	2 scruples.
Spirits of Rosemary..................	1 ounce.
Rose-water..........................	3 gills.
Wash the head once a day.	

CASTOR OIL FOR THE HAIR.

Pomade à la Rose...................	4 ounces.
Castor Oil..........................	2 ounces.
Oil of Almonds......................	2 ounces.
Essence of Bergamot.................	2 scruples.
Mix.	

ROSEMARY OIL.

Oil of Almonds......................	1 ounce.
Spirits of Rosemary...........	1 ounce.
Oil of Nutmeg.......................	18 grains.

Lawry said, "It is a rare thing to see a man entirely bald recover a full growth of hair." In a hygienic point of view, there are many excellent cosmetics that produce the desired effect when age is not the result. There are also means of preventing its fall, and preserving what remains on the head; yet there are certain cases where the loss is irreparable, and that Nature alone can remedy. In all ages, dyeing the hair was a common practice. Pliny cites a great number of cosmetic preparations employed among the Romans.

. . . *" Coma tum matatur ut annos dissimulet viridi cortice tincta nucis."*—TIBULLUS.

Myrtle baths were said to prevent baldness; also bear's oil in that as well as the present day. It was said to preserve the hair and make it grow.

Medea, the enchantress, who had the gift of rejuvenating, was probably a habile practitioner in the art of dyeing the hair.

Golden hair was then in vogue as in modern times, and the most extraordinary prescriptions were given, from a crow's liver to a swallow's dung,—and others equally curious.

Blonde hair is an appanage of a lymphatic temperament, and generally accompanies fine white skin, blue eyes, and a soft, gentle gait.

Black hair belongs to a bilious temperament and nervous disposition, and shadows a skin lightly dark, black, lively eyes, and a severe, proud gait.

Red hair accompanies a particular constitution, notwithstanding it is a blonde type. The skin of red-haired persons has a transparent freshness, and a sort of limpidity that belongs exclusively to that kind of hair. Should any one undertake to color red hair black, what expression would the eyes, so soft and languid, have with it? Experience has sufficiently established, that the preparations employed for dyeing the hair are not always free from danger. It is true these dangers have often been exaggerated. For instance, it is difficult to believe that a leaden comb poisons the hair, yet such is the result. I have seen the scalp in a dreadful state from the use of a strong dye. I have seen men and women dye their gray hair and render it purple. I have also seen ladies in despair who wished to turn their black ringlets into golden ones, obtain only a pale yellow, or a brick red. There is no doubt these strong dyes are injurious in the extreme: they break the hair, burn the scalp, and cause baldness. In spite of these results their´ use is continued.

For centuries their dangers have been exposed by excellent practitioners, and yet their use has not diminished in the least.

To-day, as in the time of Aspasia and Cleopatra, the means of embellishment are sought at any price, and no one thinks of addressing that question of Augustus to his daughter:

" Aimerais-tu mieux être chauve que blanche? "

I can recommend with confidence the following pomades:

POMADE TO DYE THE HAIR BLACK. [7]

White Wax...........................	4 ounces.
Olive Oil.....	9 ounces.
Let them dissolve, and add—Burnt cork.	2 ounces.

ANOTHER.

Powdered Nitrate of Silver............	12 grains.
Chlorohydrate of Ammonia............	12 grains.
Fresh Lard	2 ounces.
Oil of Roses............	8 drops.

Use once a day as pomade.

POWDER TO DYE THE HAIR BROWN.

Litharge	2 ounces.
Slacked Lime.......................	1 ounce.
Starch..............................	1 ounce.
Solution of Potash..................	2 drachms.

Make a homogeneal powder.

Make a paste with clear water, and apply to the head with the aid of a little brush. Cover the head with a silk night-cap, and at the end of six hours wash the hair.

POMADE TO DYE THE HAIR BLACK.

Nitrate of Silver....................	4 drachms.
Proto-nitrate of Mercury............	4 drachms.
Distilled Water.....................	1 gill.

Let it dissolve, and strain it ; add a sufficient quantity of water to obtain a solution of five ounces.

Make a paste with a sufficient quantity of starch ; bathe the hair with caution. This

3

is done on retiring. Wear a silk night-cap, and in the morning wash the hair and use any greasy substance desired.

LOTION TO PREVENT GRAY HAIR.

Vin Rouge......................	2 ounces.
Sulphate of Iron..................	18 grains.

Boil it and let it cool; use twice a week, and let it dry on the head.

TINCTURE TO COLOR THE HAIR BROWN.

Sulphur of Potassium..............	7 drachms.
Water...........................	5 ounces.
Nitrate of Silver..................	7 drachms.
Rose-water......................	7 ounces.

This liquid should be applied with the aid of a fine comb, and avoid touching the skin. This is an excellent dye, but the smell is disagreeable.

ANOTHER.

Hydrosulphur of Ammonia..........	1 ounce.
Solution of Potash................	3 drachms.
Distilled Water...................	1 ounce.

Mix well together.

Apply it on the hair with a brush for ten or fifteen minutes; continue to rub it well in the hair, separating with care the roots, so that the whole may be alike in color. Baldness is often beyond the power of art, especially when caused by age. The only visible means is the use of wigs or artificial hair, which when worn in large quantities is detrimental to health. One often sees the most youthful wigs on old men bent with age, their very wrinkles a contradiction. Any knowing eye can readily discover baldness, though covered with a luxuriant wig. The white hair would be far preferable to the latter.

I particularly allude to men, for women have so many resources, by wearing headdresses, caps, etc., that they can hide their wants in a most harmonious manner.

To resume : the hygiene of the hair consists in keeping it well brushed and cleaned, and prudently employing rational cosmetics. Seek to aid Nature, without constraining or falsifying it.

THE FOREHEAD.

"The forehead is the gate of the soul, and the temple of modesty."

THE forehead is a very important part of the face, and for physiognomists it is assuredly the most characteristic.

Lavater said, to be perfect, it should be in exact proportion with the face, equal in length with the nose and the lower part of the face. When thus exact, it produced a Grecian profile.

In size it should be either oval or square, free from irregularities and permanent wrinkles; it should, nevertheless, be susceptible of both. It should recede above, and advance below. The color of the skin should be fairer than any other part of the face. The ancient Romans looked upon a low forehead as a trait of beauty.

According to Winckelmann, the low forehead was so appropriate to all ideal heads and youthful figures of ancient art, that its form is sufficient to distinguish an ancient work from a modern one.

Evidently there are various kinds of beauty for the forehead; one cannot assuredly dissimulate the majesty attached to a high one, notwithstanding low ones are more agreeable and expressive, especially in women.

The Circassian ladies, to make their foreheads low, cut their hair, allowing it to fall over their forehead until it almost touches the eyebrows. Those who had it too high covered it with bands, thus making it low. To give the face an oval form, the hair should border the forehead enough to be round on the temples. If the forehead is hard and bony, that being its nature, it can never change; yet it contributes singularly to the varied expression of the face. There is also a mobility of the forehead, composed of the skin and muscles, that, under the action of thought, sensations, sudden emotion or grief, become contracted and wrinkled.

Its beauty does not consist alone in its size, its round or square form, but also in its majesty, severity, and grace of expression.

Permanent wrinkles in the forehead are commonly the result of age. Nevertheless they appear in youthful persons of a reflective and melancholy disposition. Some foreheads are not white nor intact : they redden under the influence of divers sentiments— modesty, shame, fright, and indignation. This is only a passing redness, but when it too easily and too frequently occurs, it produces congestion, and sometimes a painful sensitiveness.

I have seen young girls suffer so much from this redness of the forehead, that it became in time nothing less than a rush of blood to the head. True, in numerous cases it depends on the general state of the health, and is caused by an excessive degree of sensitiveness. To those afflicted, I would beg them to pay special attention to the means of preventing it.

I cannot recommend them too much to avoid prolonged attention at any study or work, especially in a position where the head is bowed. They should stop from time to time their occupation by some sudden exercise, as throwing back the shoulders, etc.

Avoid all stimulating food and drinks. Children's hair often grows down on their foreheads, so that mothers are compelled to shave it ; it is a good way to do.

At the age of puberty, young persons are afflicted with pimples and little eruptions, which are often, strange to state, excellent signs of perfect health. They disappear often without any treatment ; sometimes a little warm water and a few drops of cologne, or the following lotion :

LOTION.

Borate of Soda......................	9 grains.
Rose-water........................	5 drachms.
Orange-flower Water................	5 drachms.
For light lotion.	

Brown patches sometimes disfigure the foreheads of women especially, and particularly during pregnancy. In the last case it is but natural, and they disappear of their own accord when confinement takes place ;

in the first case they leave with difficulty, and require careful treatment.

The following prescriptions are excellent:

Chlorate of Potash....................	2 scruples.
Rose-water...........................	¼ pint.
Mix well.	

ANOTHER.

Ammonia Liquid......................	2 scruples.
Distilled Water......................	¼ pint.
Essence of Lemon....................	10 drops.
To be used on retiring.	

POMADE.

Brimstone Flour.....................	1 scruple.
Anise Oil............................	2 scruples.
Cold Cream.........................	1 ounce.
Anoint the spots on retiring, and wash with warm tea in the morning.	

As to wrinkles, I cite a few of the many formulas recommended -to diminish, if not remove them.

BALM TO DIMINISH WRINKLES.

Benzoin Water.......................	1 drachm.
White Honey........................	1 ounce.
Alcohol.............................	1 gill.

Let it macerate for eight days, then bathe the forehead lightly. A little benzoin water in pure water, with the following lotion, is also a preventive against roughness and wrinkles.

LOTION.

Turpentine	2 scruples.
Simple Water	3 ounces.]

Bathe the face and let it dry.

POMADE TO CONCEAL WRINKLES.

Essence of Turpentine	2 drachms.
Mastic	1 drachm.
Fresh Butter	2 ounces.

Mix, and use lightly.

THE NOSE.

MANY persons are constantly attacked by a partial redness of the nose, and with some it increases and becomes a reddish violet, when exposed to cold, excitement, or in drinking stimulants.

I have often seen young ladies with beau-

3*

tiful, fair skin, of lymphatic temperaments, afflicted with a slight redness at the extremity of the nose. This appeared particularly while eating, notwithstanding the food was plain and simple. I have also seen cases where the skin became thin and exfoliated at different intervals, in the form of a membrane or an onion peel. This is considered a real malady, and requires long and difficult treatment.

At other times, from no apparent cause (unless it is that of wiping it too much, or picking it with the hands), it becomes swollen and inflamed.

One of the worst things is to pick the little tan spots, or secretions, commonly called "squeezing the little worms;" it is condemned by medical men. The only way to prevent them is to take proper care in the toilet. The nails are nothing less than poison to the nose; therefore the hands should be kept from it.

Lavater said, " A beautiful nose is never associated with a deformed face. A person may be homely, and have beautiful eyes;

but a fine nose is necessarily a happy analogy of traits." The ancients called it *honestamentum facei*. The nose should be regular, and in equal length to that of the forehead. It should have in the middle of its base a superficial line, appearing to divide it into two parts; the end should not be hard, fleshy, too pointed, nor too long; its outlines should be precise; the nostrils slightly hemmed. The aisles of the nose should be free and open; in this form they denote, it is said, great delicacy of sentiment, that might easily degenerate in sensuality. The nose has various forms. The Tartars have generally flat ones; the Africans, snubby and thick; the Jews, aquiline, and remarkably long; the English, cartilaginous, and rarely pointed. The negligence of nurses is often the cause of rendering the noses of children flat, turned-up, etc. This is an assertion that one may naturally accept and say nothing in opposition. The nose is an organ that has the privilege of being more exposed than any other on the face.

The nose, with many persons, is the seat of

little black spots, especially in the sides; and sometimes are so thick, they give a disagreeable expression to the face.

Naturally, the first advice to give, is to cease habits that cause this disagreeable annoyance.

Above all, avoid the habit (so common) of squeezing them with the nails, for it causes redness and swelling of the nostrils, and often leads to serious pain. Avoid all unnecessary pomades; use only some lotion or an astringent.

The following used morning and night will prove beneficial.

LOTION.

Carbonate of Soda..................	2 scruples.
Distilled Water...........	½ pint.
Essence of Roses..................,.....	6 drops.

To be used in the morning.

Some persons have a skin so delicate and tender that they cannot wipe the nose with other than a silk handkerchief. This I do not approve of; silk or cotton are both objectionable; pure linen is the best. I give this as a hygienic precaution. Cotton irritates and produces pimples.

Many persons are provoked by the too long growth of hairs in the nostrils. It is a dangerous thing to pull them out; the best way is, when they pass the edge of the nostrils, to cut them slightly with a scissors.

THE EYEBROWS.

" There is nothing that so embellishes the body or causes one to love, as the eyes."

THE eyebrows are two rows of fine hair in the form of an arch, that rise above the eyes at the extremity of the forehead. The part nearest the nose is called the head, and the end the tail. The space between the two *entre-cil*. The eyebrows, to be handsome, should be well-furnished with hair, moderately thick, curved, and form a line in the shape of an arch. The head should have more hair than the tail,

and the numerous short hairs should lie in
and out. The two eyebrows should never
meet, and though one often sees them perfectly united, it is at the present day looked
upon as a deformity. Ovid considered it
an advantage ; but everybody has his own
opinion. Certain persons consider it a sign
of a hard disposition.

It is impossible to offer a definite remedy
for them, but with daily care they may dissimulate the disadvantage of being too thick
or too thin.

Like the hair, the eyebrows require varied
care in the toilet, according to their condition. They may be either too moist or too
dry ; and often, like the hair, they fill up
with little crusty membranes, so dry that they
cause the hair to fall, and leave the eyebrows
bare and irregular. Pass a comb carefully
over them night and morning, commencing at
the head part and following to the end, so
as to retain the shape so essential to their
beauty. A soft tooth-brush dipped in pure
water with a little cologne is quite sufficient.
When these little dry membranes or pimples

appear, dip the brush in the following mixture and pass it lightly over them :

Chlorate of Potassium	9 grains.
Pure Glycerine	1 ounce.
Water	1 gill.

When too moist, wash them with the following :

Borate of Soda	9 grains.
Distilled Water	1 gill.
Essence of Portugal	18 grains.

If they continue to fall, anoint them on retiring with a little almond oil, and in the morning wash them in tepid water.

To increase the growth of the hair on the eyebrows, it is commendable to shave them and anoint with a little sweet-oil. This means may prove useless, especially if it is in the nature of the hair to fall, having once been full. The following wash is excellent, and in some cases productive of much good :

Sulphate of Quinine	5 grains.
Alcohol	1 ounce.

To those who have very heavy eyebrows,

which is, on the contrary, more agreeable than otherwise, they should by all means avoid the habit of shaving or cutting them too close : if the hairs grow too long cut the ends lightly with a scissors.

To render them black and brown, there are various means. The simplest one to render them black is to touch them with a little black of mastic ; great care should be taken not to let it stain the fingers or skin. To darken them the following is excellent :

Gall Nuts	1 ounce.
Oil	3 ounces.
Mix with Ammoniac Salt	1 drachm.
Add a little vinegar.	

Bathe them, and let it remain on all night. Wash in the morning with tepid water.

TO RENDER THEM BROWN.

Lead Filings	1 ounce.
Iron Dust	1 ounce.
Vinegar	1 pint.

Boil all together till reduced to half the original quantity. Shake it well when cool, and wash the brows.

THE EYES.

HE eyes, above all parts of the body, paint our most secret thoughts. The eye belongs to the soul more than any other organ. It is the sense of the mind and the tongue of intelligence.

The most ordinary colors in the eyes are orange and blue; and often these two colors can be seen in the same eye. The handsomest eyes are those that appear black or blue, the lids pinkish white, not too large nor too thin, and barely passing the orb of the eye in order to give a delicate shade to the lashes, and have the white of the eye quite clear.

The eyes are most beautiful when the lashes are long and heavy, but the true beauty of the eye is in its expression. They are very fine when the angles are long and acute, especially in a horizontal direction, the lids covering a part of the white and leaving the centre of the eye clear and transparent.

Small, sparkling black eyes are very pretty when the lashes are full. The eyes should not be too round nor too prominent; when they are full, or as above, acute in form, they possess great force and an attractive gentleness.

Guyon, who wrote many works on human anatomy and physiology, said, "Whoever has received from his God the precious gift of strong, beautiful eyes, should carefully preserve them." But how few do! It is deplorable to see the negligence and forgetfulness of the hygiene of the sight.

It would be an error to believe that the mysteriously admirable expression makes its beauty. Without speaking of the changes that serious illness causes, it is sufficient to signalize its redness, fatigue, and weakness. Then taking care of the eyes is the true means of preserving the charm of their expression.

Long hours of study, reading, and work, above all for persons of lymphatic temperament, make the lids red and swollen, and often brings on tearfulness. The most minute care should be taken of young children—never to place them where their faces would be exposed to the direct influence of the light; children often, when in their cradles, and exposed to a strong light, blink and become cross-eyed.

The celebrated Arthur Chevalier notes a simple cause of squinting: it is the provoking habit of letting the hair fall over the forehead into the eyes, thus giving a false direction to the vision.

Who has not seen some little darling, while crying, rub its little hands across the eyes and brush the straying hair that clouds its face and clings to the tear-stained cheeks?

A sudden passage from obscurity to a bright light is very bad. A sleeping-room should never be very dark. Exposing the eyes to a sudden light when awakened from a long sleep, is also injurious. Care should be taken to moderate the light gradually. Careful mothers and faithful nurses will not neglect or omit a duty so important with children.

Often in the morning the eyes are sticky

and gummed together. Rubbing to open
them is the worst thing one can do; it not
only irritates the lids and reddens the eyes,
but makes the lashes fall. Bath them for ten
minutes in cold water, and much relief will
be the result. It is far better than either
warm or tepid water. Excessive labor by
lamp, gas, or other artificial light, as well as
late hours, abuse of pleasures, etc., betrays
the eyes and makes them *cernés* and old.
The observance of hygienic rules is indispensable to preserve their strength and beauty.

As I have stated, cold water is the best
lotion for the eyes, and should be repeated
several times a day; however, when they
are fatigued and red, it is well to use some
tonic lotions more fortifying. Wash them
with rose-water, mint tea, and a few drops
of alcohól, or the following lotions:

Rose-water........................	1 gill.
Vulnerary Alcohol.................	1 drachm.

ANOTHER.

Infusion of Roses..................	3 ounces.
Citron Juice......................	6 drops.

Sulphate of Zinc..................... 4 grains.
Hydro de cyanus (blue bottle)......... 3 ounces.
    Use these lotions in the morning.

The Oriental dames, to make their eyes appear large, used a fine pencil dipped in an antimonial sulphur, or Egyptian black, and rubbed it on the lids along the angles of the eye : this made it look as they wished, large, full, and almond-shaped.

LASHES.

ONG lashes are absolutely requisite to complete the beauty of the eye. The loss of them takes away much of grace from the lids, be they ever so fine. This infirmity often accompanies absence of hair, which I have just mentioned, and called *vitiligo.* We have seen that the regrowth of the hair is not, thank God, impossible. It is often very difficult, particularly here, because the application of tonics is not so easy.

A cause not commonly known, and which, to the despair of many ladies, makes the lashes fall, is a greasy secretion that lies on the lids and sometimes dries there and breaks the hair—a malady of the lid easier to explain than remove. The principal thing required is to carefully wipe away the secretions with which they are impregnated in the morning, after sleep. In this case cold-water lotions are insufficient, and fearing to detach the hair, I would advise more active lotions.

LOTIONS.

Borax	4 grains.
Syrup of Quinces	1 drachm.
Black-cherry Water, distilled	1 ounce.

It is also well to anoint them with a little sweet-oil, because it is cooling and dissipates the secretions.

Means have been sought to make the lashes thick and long. It seems difficult, not to say impossible. The irritating applications that must be used are more disadvantageous than otherwise.

It is the same when the hair grows irregularly on the lids; there is nothing to do but to cut it patiently. This is easily done by closing the eye.

THE EARS.

L'oreille est le chemin du cœur.—Madame Deshoulières.

HE ears are true ornaments of the head. The ears, to be beautiful, should possess several qualities. They should be short, round, well-turned, with a clear, lucid, transparent color, verging on a reddish pink, particularly on the edges. They should be well attached to the head, and never so far from it as to appear drooping. They should never be covered with hair. If they are too large, there is no remedy but to relieve, as far as possible, this disagreeable imperfection by an attentive toilet. With

children much may be done to prevent this
deformity. Always avoid tying the strings
of a child's hat behind its ears. An ear, to
be pretty, should be perfectly close to the
skin. In certain countries it is a mark of
distinction to have long, pendent ears. So
fixed is this intention, that at birth the ears
are pierced, and heavy rings inserted, particularly among the women in the kingdom of
Arracan, among whom long ears are a sign
of beauty. They even passed rolls of parch-
ment through to enlarge them, so as to have
them hang down to the shoulders.

In colleges, schools, and even at home, the
habit of punishing children by wringing their
ears, is a bad one, if not a very cruel one.
Parents should stop it. Without speaking of
the grave results that may arise from it, it
hardens the skin and makes the ear droop.

To preserve and keep the ears smooth,
lucid, etc., they should be washed every
morning in pure water, with a few drops of
cologne, or, better still, lemon-juice. If there
are little hairs growing on the ears, never
pull them out; it is far better to cut them.

Marian strongly condemns the use of the ear-syringe and throwing cold water too suddenly in the ear. . The Spanish and Italian ladies tinge the edges of their ears with pale pink.

THE MOUTH AND TEETH.

Vos lèvres sont rouges comme une petite bande d'écarlate. . . . Vos dents blanches et nettes sont semblables aux troupeaux de brebis que l'on vient de tondre.—SALOMON, *Cantique des Cant.*

THE mouth should be small, and in laughing or speaking should be open wide enough to show four of the upper teeth, but not more than five, straight, without saliva. Much of its beauty depends upon the form of the lips, gums, and teeth.

The *lips*, to be pretty, should be neither thick nor thin, and of an incarnate vermilion ; and, in closing, the mouth should meet and form an obtuse angle in the middle and the extremity, the under lip slightly raised ;

4

and between the nose and lips there should
be a shadowy little furrow. In Guinea, the
girls, to appear beautiful, use artificial means
to increase the size of their lips. This is,
nevertheless, very unpleasing.

Gaping lips, which give the visage such a
singular air, arise from the bad habit of keeping the mouth open and putting the fingers
in it incessantly. It should be sternly opposed.

The skin of the lips is extremely thin, especially among young persons, whose skin is
easily chapped by the wind, cold, etc.

This results from an internal irritation of
the digestive organs, and sometimes from
bad habits.

In general, children are allowed not only
to put their fingers in their mouth, but all
sorts of things. A baleful habit that may be
attributed to grown persons, is that of biting
their lips. The result in the long run is that
they become swollen, scarred, and crusty.
I will add, it is one of the most difficult habits
to correct.

To prevent redness and swelling of the

lips, apply night and morning a little warm poultice (changing it every half hour) made of potatoes or powdered rice, or the following poultice:

Bread .... 1 ounce.
Milk........... .... 1 gill.
    Boil and press.

The following pomade is excellent:

Pulverized Starch .... 1 drachm.
Spermaceti........................ 1 scruple.
White Wax........................ 1 drachm.
Oil of Olives .... 2 drachms.

The lips are often afflicted by little bluish membranes that are accompanied by little eruptions, rendering them swollen and sore. In this case use the following alkaline pomade:

Carbonate of Soda.................. 9 grains.
White Wax........................ ¼ ounce.
Cucumber Pomade................. ½ ounce.

ANOTHER.

Carbonate of Soda................. 2 scruples.
Fresh Lard.... .... ¼ ounce.
Essence of Portugal............... 1 scruple.
    For ointment.

LOTION.

Tannin...............................	1 scruple.
Water	1 gill.
Essence of Bergamot....	6 drops.
Mix carefully.	

Dip a fine linen rag in the lotion, and apply it for several minutes to the lips. When the lips have a dry tendency, the following pomade is excellent to preserve them in a good state :

ROSE POMADE FOR THE LIPS.

Oil of Roses.......................	½ pint.
Spermaceti	1½ ounce.
White Wax.......................	1½ ounce.
Alkanet Root	1½ ounce.
Essence of Rose...................	2 drachms.

Put the wax, spermaceti, the oil à la rose, and orchanet root in a bowl or earthen pot. When dissolved, pound the root fine, and let them remain four or five hours so as to extract the color, strain through a fine muslin rag, and add the essence of rose.

CERATE À LA ROSE FOR THE LIPS.

Sweet Almond Oil...................	2 ounces.
White Wax	1 ounce.

Let it steep in an earthen pot, and add Alkanet Bark or Carmine. Tie them all up in a little bag, and let it steep until of a bright red color. Let it cool a little, and add six drops Essence of Rose.

When the lips are chapped, especially the under one, anoint them morning and night, before exposing them to cold air, with pomade *ad hoc.*

Oxide of Zinc................ .... 18 grains.
Cold Cream......................... ½ ounce.
    Mix well.

ANOTHER.

Cold Cream......................... ½ ounce.

Glycerine is also excellent.

Sometimes the lips are afflicted with a painful inflammation covered with a thick crust; in this case, one must apply tonics more active.

White Precipitate .... 6 grains.
Cold Cream .... 1 ounce.
    Anoint them.

ANOTHER.

Turbith-mineral..................... 1 scruple.
Sulphur Sublimate .... 2 scruples.
Fresh Lard .... 1 ounce.
Essence of Lemon.................... 6 drops.

The gums contribute as much to the beauty of the mouth as the lips ; they should be of a fresh vermilion color. Unfortunately, from various causes—the principal one, want of care—they alter, become pale, livid, unequal, rough, and inflamed. Independent of this case, the alteration of the gums often results from a bad state of the mouth, stomach, and other organs, that have a very important influence, although often confounded with the hygiene of the teeth. As much may be said of powders.

It is true the use of sweetmeats, without washing the mouth after eating, is very detrimental, not to the gums alone, but also to the teeth. On account of their chemical decomposition, they roughen the gums and lay bare the teeth.

Tooth-powders injure, by interposing between the gums and teeth. When the gums are pale, it is useful as well as excellent to rub them briskly, and even bleed them a little with a toothpick. This should not be habitually done.

Friction causes the blood to circulate and

gives them a natural color. This advice for the gums has little to do with the teeth. Rottenstein considered healthy, regular teeth an essential ornament of the face. Rousseau said, "A woman with fine teeth could not be ugly." The premature loss of the first teeth has a grievous influence on the beauty and preservation of the second.

The simplest means to preserve the teeth, is to brush them daily in a little soap and water, and magnesia. Children should be taught this habit at an early age ; it will then come as natural to them as washing their face or hands. The teeth should be brushed after each meal if possible ; if not, rinse the mouth with a little tepid water. Toothpicks should be elastic ; goose-quills are preferable to the metallic toothpicks. According to Rottenstein, to pass a thread between the teeth after each repast, is excellent. Tooth-brushes should be hard, but not so as to cause pain.

Among the number of dental preparations, washes are preferable to powders, although a great many of the latter are excellent ; charcoal for instance, though hurtful to the gums, is excellent for the teeth. In any case, powders should not be constantly used. But above all things to be avoided are acids. They make the teeth white at the expense of the enamel. Lemons are also injurious, although ladies use them a great deal, by rubbing the peel on their teeth and gums to make the one white and the other red, which often results in caries, that cruel enemy of the mouth.

It is an excellent habit to clean the teeth on retiring, with a little pure water and soap. Avoid breaking nuts or other hard substances with them. I would caution women, in particular, to avoid breaking their threads with them.

Hot or cold water should never be used; a little tepid is the best. The following prescriptions, according to tastes and habits, may be used with success:

POWDER.

Precipitate Chalk......................	1 pound.
Powdered Starch......................	½ pound.
Iris Powder........................	¼ pound.
Sulphate of Quinine.................	1 scruple.

    Pass it through a sieve.

POWDER.

Precipitate Chalk...................... 4 ounces.
Borax Powder......................... 2 ounces.
Myrrh............................... 1 ounce.
Iris .... 1 ounce.
    Mix.

POWDER.

Charcoal ....⎫
Peruvian Bark...............⎬ Of each, 2 drachms.
Iris Powder........................ 1 scruple.
    Mix.

In using these powders, always rinse the mouth with lukewarm water.

VIOLET WATER FOR THE TEETH.

Tincture of Iris............⎫
Spirits of Roses............⎬ Of each, equal parts.
Alcohol ....⎭

ANOTHER.

Brandy............................ ½ gill.
Alcohol, Vulnerary .... ½ gill.
Oil of Mint........................ 18 grains.
    Mix well.

ANOTHER.

Brandy............................ 1 scruple.
Soap Water........................ 2 scruples.
Tincture of Pyrethrum.............. 9 grains.
    Mix with water, and use a tooth-brush.
2*

ANOTHER.

Eau de Cologne........................ 1 pint.
Myrrh .... 1 gill.
　Let it steep fifteen days, then strain.

OPIATE FOR THE TEETH.

Honey.............................. 4 ounces.
Chalk.............................. 4 ounces.
Iris ...:........................... 4 ounces.
Carmine............................ 1 scruple.
Essence of Cloves.................. 9 grains.
Essence of Nutmeg................. 9 grains.
Essence of Roses.................. 9 grains.
Syrup...................... quantity sufficient.

The simplest prescription is pure water, but when the breath is bad, it is indispensable to use some tonic or wash. To remove any disagreeable odor arising from the breath, caused by eating onions, cabbage, etc., it is sufficient to take a little black coffee, fresh nuts, or orange-flower tea.

For those who smoke, there are many agreeable remedies. The following lozenges are good and easily made :

TURKISH LOZENGES.

White Sugar	2 pounds.
Citric Acid	2 drachms.
Essence of Roses	5 drops.
Musk in grains	4 grains.
Essence of Vetiver	14 grains.

Mix as a paste, putting a little solution of Adragant Gum in the water and color it. Let it become hard, then cut at will.

Let us add, a gracious smile gives additional charm to the beauty of the mouth, so that the manner of smiling has an extreme importance. Too much cannot be said against a loud, coarse laugh. A soft, gentle smile is becoming to women, especially when they open their mouth a little, and produce two little dimples; while the under lip should cover the extremity of the upper teeth, to render the laugh lovely. Ovid said, "That since his time, the beautiful had learned to laugh."

" *Quis credat discunt etiam ridere puella.*"

THE CHEEKS.

ROPERLY speaking, the cheeks unite the two parts of the visage that lose themselves in lines more or less marked, and aided by the play of the muscles, they principally form the physiognomy. From them arise the various expressions that paint the sensations which express themselves by movement, form, and color. They are thin or fleshy, hollowed or gently rounded, rosy or pale, smooth or intersected by light traces and little wrinkles ; naturally graceful, they are agitated by a gentle trembling, which raises them towards the eyes. The cheeks should be smooth, slightly rounded, full and of equal size. Nothing contributes more to render the cheeks flat, than the lack of a few large teeth ; therefore one cannot be too careful of them, especially young persons.

The cheeks are from their nature the seat of the impurities that we have seen spoil the complexion. It is upon them, principally, that are seen those little white scars and red spots, so common among young children after being kissed, but which happily soon disappear.

Therefore, as Andry remarks, it is a deplorable habit to let every one kiss young children ; their tender, delicate cheeks should be respected, and one should be content to kiss the forehead gently, or better still, the little hands.

Many persons, especially those of a lymphatic temperament whose cheeks appear swollen, are what is called chubby-cheeked. Without that, it implies an infirmity.

In this inflated condition I have often seen young girls, having not only their cheeks, but the upper lip, and even the eyes, appear covered. This condition, almost a malady, frequently disappears of itself at the age of puberty, but too often remains independent of medical means and hygienic precautions, all of which are indispensable to be used. These means consist in taking care to avoid isolation, the light of a strong fire, and the action of a cold wind. Gymnastic exercises, and all that tends to increase the activity of the circulation, are commendable. Avoid all sedentary occupations, and eat plain food. As to tonics, they produce little effect.

The skin in some cases is fresh, white, and delicate, and cannot support pomades, unless very mild. In this case dip a little linen rag in cologne water and bathe the face. When perfectly dry, use a little powdered starch. This is an excellent precaution for young persons when exposed to a cold or humid wind, but they should avoid riding in open carriages.

THE CHIN.

HE under lip, says Herder, begins the chin, and the jawbone descending on each side terminates it. It may be looked upon as the real key of the edifice. According to the Greeks, it should not be pointed nor hollow, but united and insensible. The chin is often covered with pimples, which in men is caused by shaving and the growth of the beard. To avoid this, one should shave daily with a good razor and warm water ; then wash the chin several times with cold water and a few drops of cologne, always wiping slowly with a fine towel. Those who wish to wear the beard long should never forget to brush and comb it several times a day, sometimes bathing it in a little perfumed liquor.

CHAPTER II.

BEAUTY OF THE FACE—Resumed.

E have seen in detail the traits which contribute to the beauty and physiognomy of the face. The air of the visage is an essential part of respectability.

A modest, gracious, enchanting air is ordinarily expressive of an honest, gentle, peaceful soul. It impresses on the brow a noble, majestic disposition; in the eye, candor and cordiality. From that air comes gentleness, affability, and in a word, the most beautiful expression resulting from a pure mind and a good heart. But is not the physiognomy deceitful? Yes. It can be remade. Nevertheless, paint is never the skin itself, be it ever so adroitly applied.

The skin on the face is remarkable for its mobility, resulting from numerous physical and moral causes ; this change is due to the variety of individual expression, principally dependent on the disposition, habits, and professions. It is well known, that this flexibility of face has made the talent and reputation of the greatest comedians, who succeeded in attaining it by perseverance and study. Grimaces are but exaggerated expressions and movements of the muscles. One cannot begin too early to oppose this bad habit among children. And I may also address a few observations to grown people, who amuse themselves making wry faces before children ; it is a nervous influence that guides the muscular movements of the face. It is hardly credible the influence that imitation exercises on the nervous movements of the face. The pleasantness of the face consists less in the particular form of its traits, than in the harmony and mobility which constitute their expression. The expression of the face depends above all on the sentiments of the soul. Transitory, they leave but a transient impression. Others contracted daily in a good or bad education impress themselves profoundly : thus anger, pride, and scorn produce the most disagreeable airs.

The skin on the face is also remarkable for its fine delicate structure and sensibility. From these arise the changes of color under the influence of divers impressions.

Sometimes pimples, spots, and other alterations in its color, betray a modification of the state of health or disease. Outside of any sickly state, the colors of the skin on the face are so special, that there is nothing more difficult for a painter than to make an image of them, and he cannot do it without mixing separately all the colors in his palette.

THE FORM.

F, as we have said, real beauty—the beauty which charms and seduces—resides principally in the visage, it is, however, only one part of the subject we propose to treat. One cannot conceal in view of its connection with the embellishment of the body, the interest which the study of the figure properly called members, etc., presents.

A graceful form gives a remarkable ease to the carriage, a light attitude and gentleness that add singularly to the power of beauty. "Learn to walk as becomes a woman," said Ovid. There is in the step a grace that is not to be disdained.

" *Est et in incessu pars non temnenda decoris.*"

There is in the step a certain distinction which will be found well explained in the History of England and Scotland. The author in speaking of Anne Boleyn, the wife of Henry VIII., said, "She had in her

appearance and manner a charming and in-
imitable air."

Winckelmann, in his History of Antiquity,
says: The Greeks sought to observe great
modesty in their carriage and actions.   They
believed that a precipitate step shocked the
ideas of propriety, and announced a sort of
rusticity in the manners.

—————————

THE NECK.

HE backbone is that flexible column
which extends from the neck to the
inferior extremity of the reins.   When
it is straight, supple, and well placed, it
makes, with the aid of the neck, shoulders,
breast, and hips, a beautiful waist.

· The neck is the commencement of the
breast ; among women it is rounded.   Bernardin de St. Pierre called it a cylindrical
column, in his studies on nature.

To be well made, it should be slightly

rounded, long, moderately slender, and well detached from the shoulder. A well-formed neck is one of the most agreeable features of the human species.

THE SHOULDERS.

THE shoulders have also their kind of beauty. With women they are less removed from the trunk; they should be level, well-posed, large, and insensibly descending.

THE CHEST.

THE chest should be large, well raised, and gracefully rounded. To be well-placed, the breasts should have an interval between, equal to that which exists between the nipples and the middle of the hollow of the collar-bones. They should be slightly rounded, little, hard, and not too much attached to the body. Women have the collar-bones less curved, and consequently longer, which gives them ordinarily large and beautiful width. Women have the abdomen fuller, the waist finer, and the hips more advanced than men. To render the waist small, large hips are a natural necessity. The waist is considered the pivot of the divers movements of the body. It constitutes that grace which La Fontaine has proclaimed, *" Plus belle que la beauté."* One sees, indeed, every day, women with pretty faces, and yet, from their clumsy, thick waist, they fail to attract ; while others, less beautiful, with irregular traits, please and attract by their slender waist and graceful carriage. The waist, properly speaking, marks the regions of the back and the loins. In well-formed women, the waist is generally long, and remarkable for its flexibility and elegance.

Andry notes numerous alterations to which the waist is subject, as well as the cares and precautions it requires from infancy. From his singular work I borrow a few useful hints which have merited success, although too neglected at the present day. "It is no easy task," says he, "in the education of children, to care as much for the mind as for the body. There are very few perfect waists. The shoulders are either round, the neck is too short, or one shoulder is higher and larger than the other, or inclines too much to the side; all these conditions tend to disfigure the waist. When the shoulders of a young girl have a tendency to roundness, she should frequently exercise her arms by throwing them behind, posing them over the hips so as to advance the chest. She should sleep on her back. I have often seen young ladies who had this vicious tendency, wear a kind of corset with braces two or three hours every day, so as to bring the shoulders back in place, and enlarge the chest. Orthopedic corsets are excellent. To prevent children from bending their neck, there are a host of means, many of which are very simple, such as tying elastic bands, etc.

Another point to which I would call attention is : Never place a child in a cradle where its head is turned towards the light. Another bad habit is taking children up by their hands, or dancing them up in the air, to "see their grandfather." This playful custom is injurious, and one runs the risk of deforming the carriage of the head.

To prevent the neck from sinking between the shoulders, one should take children up by the waist. Later, when children are studying, their desk or table should be two fingers lower than their elbows, but not too low. If too low, it forces them to advance their shoulders; if too high, it compels them to raise them too much. It is the same for a dining-table. Young children should not be tied in their chairs; if tied, place a little footstool under their feet. The manner of wrapping up a child contributes much to this defect. Lay the body straight, the arms even with the legs. Never carry a child constantly on the same arm. If one shoulder inclines to the side, numerous precautions are given, which apparently possess no great value, but are not, however, without importance. Constant exercise will contribute to correct this deformity.

THE WAIST.

STOUT waist requires hygienic care, activity, and great exercise. The same of one that is too slight. Do not confound this with a waist too small—that is to say, reduced to such proportions as are incompatible with health. And here I cannot too strongly condemn the frequent habit that young persons have, of tight-lacing, to make their waists small. They commit a great error; for the beauty of the waist does not consist in its size, but in the harmonious bearing of all the parts that concur to form it. It is also seriously detrimental to health. I have seen many unfortunate results, serious, and even mortal accidents, from this practice. Sometimes the waist is all one piece; nothing easy or

5

free. Notwithstanding its fine mould, it has a constrained air, which seems as if the person had a sword down the back. All kinds of exercise are recommended that oblige children to leap, run, etc., so as to develop and render flexible the limbs.

To prevent the waist from turning, Andry recommended various means, which are employed up to the present day. A very important matter is too little regarded : it is the choice of little chairs used for young children.

The seat should be narrow and close, because, if soft-bottomed, it sinks in the centre so that the child when seated has a tendency to bend its neck. This deformity is attended by general causes, debility, etc. Andry goes so far as to recommend chairs with wooden bottoms and side pieces, so as to make them high or low at will.

It is important that young girls, during their work or study, should constantly preserve a straight posture, nevertheless without a disagreeable stiffness. Thus, in reading or sewing, they should hold their work or book towards the eyes, rather than their eyes towards them. Another recommendation : they should not forget, when occupied at the piano, or painting, to sit up straight. For a long time we have noted the disadvantages of tight shoes, that wound the feet, and finish by altering the carriage, and above all the position of the waist. High heels make young people stoop.

The want of solidity, equilibrium, assurance, and rectitude in the step, are causes that easily change the waist.

Corsets demand the greatest care in their make. God be thanked, at the present day, those steels and whalebones, so injurious to the bodies of young persons, are renounced. Moderately easy to support, they should never press closely the front of the chest, particularly the breasts.

With those who are growing, great care should be taken to change the size as the form develops. A very tight corset worn for eight days may spoil a waist.

An easy corset should be two fingers wide across the upper part of the chest, to leave

loose space for the breasts. Corsets are indispensable to young persons of a delicate
constitution.

THE ARMS.

EAUTIFUL arms are characteristic
of women. To be beautiful, they
should be round, plump, small at
the wrist, and gracefully taper towards the
elbows.

THE HANDS.

EAUTIFUL hands are a charm, but
they are rare.

Among the lower classes of women,
beautiful eyes, mouth, and forehead are
common, but rarely beautiful hands. This
is easily understood, if one reflects on the
care they require, and the hard work these

women are obliged to perform. Organs of tact, endowed as they are with an exquisite sensibility in contact with so many exterior objects, they evidently require the most minute care.

A well-shaped hand should be delicate, a little long, and smooth, so that the veins in the back should not appear too large. Little dimples at the extremity of each finger should appear when the hand is open. The fingers should be long and tapering. This form, when it gradually diminishes, is very agreeable, and makes them appear like little columns of lovely proportions. To possess an agreeable form, the hands should be a little rounded, the thumb reach half-way up the first finger when the hand is open or closed, and the first finger should reach the nail of the second ; while the middle finger should be a nail's length longer than either ; the third should not be quite a half a nail's difference with the centre ; and the little finger should reach the second joint of the third.

The hollow of the hand, when open, should be dimpled and full ; the skin should be white, fine, and soft, with numerous imperceptible lines ; while the fingers should possess a supple, flexible air.

THE NAILS.

THE beauty of the finger-nails consists in their pinky tint and well-rounded edge and smooth surface.   The free portion of the nail should be short and round.   If allowed to grow too long it points, and ends by bending itself on the pulp of the finger.   Excessively long nails are considered a sign of beauty by the Chinese ; by us they are considered a sign of slovenliness.

"Et nihil emineant sint sordibus ungues."

"Que les ongles ne soient pas trop longs et qu'ils soient exempts de tout ordure."

Their cleanliness is, in fact, one of the most indispensable cares of the toilet.   Unless they are clean and neat, they are no more beautiful hands than a pretty mouth with dirty teeth.

The nails, from their transparency, present a brilliant tissue color, sometimes bluish, on account of the state of the health, disease, etc. The Persians are so fond of rosy nails, they tint and paint them. The Indians often do the same.

The beauty of the hands, when perfect, is a great ornament. Although there are few persons who possess that advantage, they may by special care attain it.

ROUGHNESS OF THE HANDS.

DEFORMITY, or rather a disadvantage, commonly seen, is roughness of the hands. Instead of being soft and flexible, the skin is rough and unequal, particularly with those who are given to manual labor, and whose hands come in contact with hard substances. There are, of course, various exceptions. I have seen ladies who never did any labor, whose hands were by nature red, rough, and dry. This is sometimes augmented by exposure to cold, constant use of warm or cold water, and irritating soap. When the hands are thus afflicted, care should be taken to pro-tect them from the cold. Wash them in luke-warm water and mild soap. Bran water and almond paste are excellent. Anoint them with a little cold cream, and wear gloves on retiring. Avoid manual labor, if possible, and, above all, do not wet them too much.

ALMOND PASTE.

Bitter Almonds, peeled.............	½ pint.
Honey.............................	1 pint.
Yolk of Eggs.......................	2 drachms.
Sweet Almond Oil..................	1 pint.
Essence of Bergamot...............	2 drachms.
Essence of Cloves..................	2 drachms.

Beat the honey and the yolks of the eggs together; add the oil little by little, then the almonds and essences.

POWDER TO WHITEN HANDS.

Horse-chestnuts, pounded . . . . 10 ounces.
Bitter Almonds. . . . . 9 ounces.
Iris Powder. . . . . 1 ounce.
Carbonate of Potash. . . . . 2 drachms.
Essence of Bergamot. . . . . 1 drachm.

> Mix. Put a little in two or three glasses of water and wash the hands.

COSMETIC GLOVES FOR THE HANDS.

Yolk of Fresh Eggs. . . . . 2 scruples.
Sweet Almond Oil. . . . . 2 tablespoonfuls.
Rose-water. . . . . 1 ounce.
Tincture of Benzoin. . . . . 36 grains.

Beat the yolks up with the oil, and add successively the rose-water and the tincture. Put this inside the gloves, and sleep in them.

CHAPS AND CRACKS ON THE HANDS.

THE skin on the hands cracks and chaps, covering the hands with lines which are exceedingly painful.

To those thus afflicted, I recommend them

5*

not to wash their hands too often, and above all, when they do, to take the greatest care in wiping them ; half the time the neglect in drying them causes the chap.

I have often noticed that musicians accustomed to frequent exercise at the piano, and even young beginners at that instrument, suffer a keen pain in their fingers.

A means that has been used with good effect is the following

MIXTURE.

Tincture of Aloes...............	1 to 3 scruples.
Glycerine......................	1 ounce.

On retiring, anoint the fingers and wear gloves. It is simple and easily mixed.

ANOTHER FOR CHAPPED HANDS.

Spermaceti	18 grains.
Olive Oil..........................	2 drachms.
White wax.........................	4 drachms.

Mix carefully, and according toart.

The back of the hand has numerous veins that should barely appear, but with many persons they swell, and become voluminous ;

and be the hand ever so fine, they look rough when the veins are large. It is almost impossible to suggest a remedy that can prevent their swelling. However, a few hints as precautions may be given.

First, never wash them in hot water. Avoid tight sleeves—gloves can be worn a little tight.

Many young persons, particularly those of a lymphatic temperament, suffer from chilblains in the fingers and hands, that often result in destroying the color of the skin, and leave scars and reddish-blue marks.

The following pomades are highly praised :

POMADE.

Opium............................	2 drachms.
Powdered Sulphur..................	1 drachm.
Carbonate of Ammonia..............	2 drachms.
Acetate of Lead...................	4 drachms.
Fresh Lard.......................	4 ounces.

ANOTHER.

Essence of Turpentine.............	1 drachm.
Olive Oil........................	2 drachms.
Sulphuric Acid...................	18 grains.

The hands are also subject to little excrescences, that assume various forms, and are known under the name of warts. Their presence has something repugnant; it is probably because general opinion deems them contagious.

A number of means to destroy them has been proposed. The best method is to tie a silk thread tight around the wart—that is, if its base is not too closely grown on the hand. They can also be cut off or cauterized on the surface. Medical works on the subject deny that the blood of a wart dropping on the hand will produce others.

Nitrate of silver (or pierre infernal) is good. Caustics are dangerous when badly applied.

A small quill dipped in a little muriatic acid is a slow but not disagreeable application.

Another disagreeable feature is sweaty hands. I have seen young people so troubled with these, that they were constantly wiping them with their handkerchief, especially in the palm; perspiration so powerful in its nature, that it would stain gloves, silk, or anything of color it touched. Evidently linked to some particular individual cause, it increases under the influence of heat, rapid movements, or moral emotions.

It is an infirmity difficult to remove. It is, however, prudent to abstain from the use of astringents ; there is only one local means, and that is the use of powdered starch.

Means have been used to turn the sweat to the feet by the use of flannel, but as we shall soon see, the perspiration of the feet is far more disagreeable than that of the hands.

General means are the best to oppose this weakness. Much depends on the constitution and the food.

Regular exercise, riding horseback, gymnastics, etc., tend to diminish it.

Tonics are excellent.

Thermal baths are the best, because they have direct action on the skin. The waters of Cauterets de Bagnères, Luchon, Barèges, Uriage, Schinsnach, etc. Sea-bathing by its reaction produces the same effect. Dr. John-

son, one of the first American physicians of
Paris, has treated successfully many difficult
cases of skin diseases, and recommends the
waters of Spa, also Pierrefoulis; the latter is
most salutary.

The first condition of the nails is cleanliness. Between the nails and the skin are
fatty secretions, resulting from the impurities
with which we come in contact. This fatty
substance is always of a black nature. This
disagreeable effect is so marked, that even
with the minute care that some persons give,
they cannot keep them clean; and in endeav-
oring to remove it, they only press it deeper
into the extremity of the nail. This is often a
double cause why some persons always have
dirty nails.

To clean the nails, it is sufficient to use a
brush and soap. The brush should be full,
large, and soft. Some persons keep them exceedingly neat, it is true, by rubbing the
extremity of the fingers with verjuice or
lemon. If the liquid flows on the surface of
the nail (which it is impossible to prevent),
in point of beauty, the process is not with-

out disadvantage, as I will plainly show. The nail, to be beautiful, should be well bordered with the skin on all sides; the tender film should be intact; therefore great pains should be taken not to rub it too hard. Nothing injures it so much as the contact of the acids that I have already mentioned. Hot water is also injurious.

One can regulate the borders of the nails by passing daily a little steel-pointed file around them. It sometimes happens, however, that the membrane at its base extends on the nail so far as to cover the " half moon," or little white crescent, which is one of the marks of beauty of a perfect nail. It should be raised with great precaution with the point of the nail file.

Long nails are a great defect, because at the extremity they break, produce pain, and sometimes cause severe inflammation. The same may be said of a nail cut too short, causing nervous irritation and analogous effects. There are many persons who do not give the nails a chance to grow, but cut them, and bite them with their teeth—a frightful habit. The result is, the nail loses its strength, and ends by breaking. Others end by being surmounted by the flesh at the extremities of the fingers, rendering the nail in the form of a pad ; it is very ugly, and the habit, once formed, it is difficult to correct this deformity. The pad itself is an obstacle to the growth of the nail, and becomes painful. If one should decide to let it grow anew, it should be bound round with little bands of cloth dipped in diachylon gum. But in spite of all this, the nail will continue to grow large and unequal.

However, one should endeavor to render the surface of the nails smooth, by mechanically but lightly using a fine ivory nail press.

The nails may be polished by rubbing with a sponge dipped in an equal mixture of cinnabar and pulverized emery, and afterwards passing a little oil of bitter almonds over them.

The nail sometimes loses its transparency in several places, becoming the seat of little white spots disagreeable to the view. The French call these "little lies." Fortunately, however, the nail in growing (for there is no other means) makes them disappear. As to the accidental or superficial stains that fruit or nutshells have upon the fingers or nails, they may be removed by a little lemon-juice, or some steeped laurel leaves. Sometimes pure water without soap will remove them.

Many persons are obliged to cut their nails short on account of the easy manner in which they break. The cause of this is the general dryness of the skin, and can only be remedied by local means. For instance, anoint them in the evening with pure mutton, lotion, or cold cream, and the following pomade :

Tar...............................	18 grains.
Hog's Lard.......................	1 ounce.
Mix.	

Rub the hands and nails with it, and glove them over night; wash thoroughly in the morning with soap and warm water, or a little rosemary tea.

Sometimes, near the root of the nail, little pieces of flesh become detached and are very painful. Many persons are constantly subject to them, especially in cold weather. In

order to prevent them, one should avoid
rubbing the hands against irritating or corro-
sive substances. They should never be pulled
off, for that only produces pain and inflammation, and at times has caused onychia. Cut
them with a sharp scissors or knife, and put
on a little court plaster.

THE THIGHS AND LEGS.

THE thighs are principally remarkable
among women for their fulness, the
beauty of their outlines, and their
polish. They should be firm, massive, and
slightly touch each other above the knees.

Moreau de la Saithe, the celebrated author,
said that the reliefs which support them behind had a type of beauty that would be
difficult to describe. Dryness and exaggeration are the ordinary defects of these parts.

Legs are handsome when long, round,
tapering, white, and free from hair. An ele-

gantly formed calf should curve with grace from the ankle to the knee; also as it approaches the thighs. The knee, joints should show slightly.

THE FEET.

THE feet, like the hands, have an expression of beauty entirely their own. The foot should be large or small, according to the proportion of the body ; but white, round, and well placed. The heel should be neither too flat nor too high. Modern shoes differ much from ancient ones, and arrest the development of the foot by their ridiculous compressions. Ladies should always wear their shoes longer than their feet, so as to maintain ease and grace in their movements. In general ladies torture themselves to have a small foot : 'tis a mistake ; a little foot is not pretty. Others injure their feet by wearing shoes too large. Feet, like the hands, are susceptible to many deformi-

ties : they have their specialties. To prevent
these deformities there are various means.
The feet above any part of the body require
care, especially in warm weather. Frequent
change of stockings, and washing them in pure
lukewarm water and soap, are the simplest
means. For those who walk a great deal
and perspire, rub them with a little alcohol
and water or cologne.

Frederick the Great introduced surgeons
into his army, whose duty it was to survey
the soldiers' feet. The scarfskin, in persons
who walk a great deal, often becomes hard,
dry, and very thick. It is well to anoint the
soles of the feet with some greasy substance,
as this thickness often becomes painful, and
sometimes causes a deformation. It also
produces what is called callosity and corns.
Both are generally the result of compression
produced by tight shoes, or the slipping of
shoes that are too large.

Camper has fully noted the conditions
that shoes should possess. He has shown
the necessity of accommodating their form to
the feet, their changes and movements. The

callosity which forms on the soles and heels of the feet of persons who walk a great deal, when softened, becomes exceedingly painful, and impedes the step. The difference between corns and callosity is, one rests upon the surface, while the other, in a horny root, penetrates the flesh. As I have just said, it is sufficient in this case to anoint them with a little greasy substance, and rest. Corns have deep roots. Celsus called them "foot nails," on account of the excessive pain they occasion, especially when they grow between the great toes. Corns are an alteration of the epidermis on the feet when shoes too large or too small are worn. They are sometimes produced by folds or plaits in the stocking, which are often too large. Persons with a fine, delicate, sensitive skin are more subject than those whose skin is insensible and thick.

Corns grow insensibly, and only become painful when of a certain size. They are sometimes accompanied by a redness and swelling of the toe, and always by a sharp pain, which is aggravated by the least contu-

sion. Cut them with a scissors, a razor, or
chip them round with a little blunt instrument *ad hoc,* so as to remove the thick dry
skin ; or, better still, pull them off with the
nails, after having softened them by a plaster
or poultice of diachylon gum, soft wax, or a
foot-bath. This is often the most palliative,
as well as most generally employed, and is
more soothing than the others. Corns take
more or less time to grow, so that one may
recommence treatment when necessary. A
more active means—perhaps too active, because it may prove dangerous—is the use of
caustics, potassium, hydrochloride of ammonia, nitric and sulphuric acids, etc. Badly
employed, they often penetrate deeper than
they should, and before one can moderate
their action, cause grave accidents. The best
and only curative means is extirpation.
Use a blunt needle-handle *ad hoc,* and penetrate the corn, after having cut all around it.
A good corn-cutter can penetrate the root of
the corn without causing a drop of blood to
flow, or exciting the least pain. Emollient
baths, though not agreeable before this oper-

ation, are very useful after; at least, if the feet have not been washed in alkalized water, which is just as good. A multitude of means are recommended for curing corns—plasters of soap, mucilage, ammoniac gum, galbanum, and all kinds of adhesive plasters, sea-green leaves, etc. In spite of their success, they merit little confidence, but as they are not dangerous, they may be employed by those who fear to yield to a corn-doctor. Corns may even be cured by wearing comfortable shoes.

GOLDEN CERATE FOR CORNS.

Yellow Wax.........................	5 ounces.
Sulphate of Zinc...	1 ounce, 3 drachms, 18 grains.
Oxide Copper............	3 drachms, 2 scruples.
Verdigris.................	3 drachms, 2 scruples.
Borax....................	3 drachms, 2 scruples.
Red Chalk........	1 ounce, 3 drachms, 18 grains.

After a long, fatiguing walk, the feet, especially the heels, are affected by a little white blister full of serosity, looking like a bulb produced by a burn. It is a passing inconvenience. Prick it carefully, and let the water out without breaking the skin ; apply a little linen cloth with cold cream, and refrain from long walks. This is simple, and sufficient to cure it.

Bunions.—The feet are often burdened with blisters of another nature and more difficult to cure, called bunions, which come generally on the joint of the great toe, and often become hard as the bone itself. Frequent foot-baths, soft plasters, and easy shoes relieve them. A little cushion of cotton wool placed between them and the shoes is also a means of relief.

Chilblains.—I have already spoken of the hands as being painfully deformed by chilblains, but they are far more frequent and injurious in the feet, particularly of children and young girls with delicate skin and lymphatic temperament. They sometimes constitute a real disease. To prevent chilblains from returning, as they always do in cold damp weather, use daily a lotion of pure water with snow wine or camphorated brandy. Liquid of ammonia and eau de cologne are excellent. Peruvian balm is

much praised. I have seen employed with
great advantage the following pomade :

Precipitate White	5 grains.
Chloroform	5 grains.
Cold Cream	1 ounce.

When they are very painful and swollen, apply a poultice of elder-flowers and camomile ;
or bind them with a little cerate sprinkled
with camphor. Electricity has been used for
them with success in many cases. If they
show a tendency to spread or ulcerate, these
means will prove insufficient. Then choose
a healthy air, warm clothing, strengthening
food, and exercise in walking. Cod-liver
oil, Peruvian bark, etc., are excellent to for-
tify the system. Sometimes chilblains have
an itching sensation, that is so painful, it
spreads to inflammation. For this I can only
add, use frequent foot-baths, with cologne in
the water ; or spread on a linen cloth a little
of the following pomades :

Carbonate of Lead	18 grains.
Cold Cream	1 ounce.

6

Essence of Bergamot....................	10 drops.
Sulphur Sublimate....................	18 grains.
Cerate.............	1 ounce.
Essence of Lemon....................	10 drops.

Mix with great care.

The hands and feet are sometimes covered with an excessive perspiration, particularly the latter, accompanied with a disagreeable odor. If it is accidentally produced by a long walk, the simplest care will remove it. But unfortunately it is a constant trouble to some persons, who, in spite of their habits of cleanliness and change of hose, continue to be afflicted. I say afflicted, because the odor from the feet when in that state is insufferable. To remedy it is almost impossible ; yet there are means that render it endurable without injury to the health. These means are ablutions, with infusions of sage, rosemary, thyme, etc. Bathe them morning and night, and after each bath wipe them very dry, and rub them with a little powder. Let the powder be perfumed The following are simple and excellent :

Powdered Starch...................... 1 pound.

Iris Powder........................ 4 ounces.

Camphor.......................... 2 drachms.

    Mix all together.

No. 2.

Fine White Chalk................... 1 pound.

Pulverized Starch.................. ½ pound.

Iris............................... ½ pound.

    Mix well, and rub the feet with a little.

The toe-nails require as much care as, if not more than, the finger-nails. Sometimes the gravest results arise from their malformation, which is often caused by negligence in cutting them, and by allowing them to grow too long, wearing tight shoes, and finally pressing them into the flesh, where they become rooted, and cause sharp pain. To prevent all this, the means employed are simple. Cut them in a half-circle, and not too close to the skin. If neglected, they often grow very long, and from the pressure of the shoe recede and bend in the form of a claw, and are sometimes so thick they chip off and break, causing severe pain. When the nail is naturally dry and breaks of itself, use a fine

file, and smooth it off if surrounded by a dry
secretion ; wash it in a little saleratus water,
wipe dry, and anoint with a little fresh lard
or cold cream.

THE FIGURE.

WILL not occupy myself with the
strict rules concerning the size of the
waist, but simply those that contribute
to its beauty. In all cases, it should principally consist in the size of all those parts
whose attitudes contribute to its grace and
beauty. The waist of men is generally longer than that of women, and differs according to climate. The inhabitants of the north
are generally taller than those of the south.
In effect, certain habits and certain exercises
aid the development of the form : arms,
swimming, gymnastics, etc.   The waist is
considered the medium part of the form ;
above all, among women is characteristic of

the *beau ideal.* Such was the opinion of the Greeks and Romans.

Clothing helps to show the form to advantage, or to give it grace when lacking. The ancient use of cloaks attached on one shoulder, and hiding a portion of the form, left the waist exposed, because it was such an advantage to beauty. That stiffness which is fatal to grace, is often caused by excessively tight clothing. "The limbs should be at ease in the clothing," said Rousseau. "Nothing should restrain them, nothing should tighten them or paste them to the body." It is a ridiculous pretension, and a deplorable error, to regard an extremely slender waist as very beautiful. If we consider the waist as allied with the carriage, it is one of the principal points of our subject. We will see that a pretty carriage and a fine waist are the result of a just proportion and exact bearing of all the divers parts. There are, moreover, many degrees and varieties in the beauty of the waist.

A pretty waist means a small one ; a fine waist, a large one.

In the history of Augustus, who was one of the handsomest men of his time, his fine figure is mentioned. Nevertheless, the merit of the figure consists less in its elevation or its slightness than in the just proportion that favors freedom and grace of movement. The waist should be in proportion to the bust it supports. Be that as it may, elegance, lightness, and grace of figure are essential qualities of beauty; in them dwell dignity, force, and, in a word, *tournure*.

The movements of a gentleman are always elegant, at least when not restrained by timidity, or still worse, by affectation. In walking, avoid waddling; it is a disagreeable deformity, into which many persons fall by a bad habit. There is something very disagreeable in a heavy, torpid step; it originates from want of attention in making a child walk in proportionate steps with a grown person. Never walk faster than a child; it is a bad habit to take long strides, for it causes that heavy, torpid walk so often seen. Many young persons walk as if embarrassed by their legs. Ease of support is a very important thing ; its absence suffices to leave a bad impression at first sight. "A fool," said La Bruyère, "does not enter, go out, sit, nor stand on his legs, like an intelligent man."

Without accepting that maxim as absolute, parents are recommended to prevent, if possible, that disagreeable habit.

In effect, ease of attitude, flexibility, and grace add much to the fascinations and power of beauty.

CHAPTER III.

THE SKIN.

THE skin is not only a remarkable coat that covers the outlines, more or less harmonious, of the periphery, but is composed of several distinct organs and divers membranes, that give it intimate relation with the rest of its keeping, and render it one of the most curious and important parts of the human organization. The skin is endowed with a peculiarly exquisite. tenderness. The nervous papillæ constitute a special sense; vessels that animate and color it; marvellous little organs that establish between it and the rest of the network a continual intercourse; the whole clothed with a fine, thin coating that completely protects it. It breathes, throws out all impure matters carried by the tide of circulation. In effect, it is sustained by a coating more or less thick, according to the regions of the tissue which maintains it; softening all the inequalities of the body, and facilitating its movements. When nothing occurs to alter this miscellaneous condition, the skin seems to have life in itself. Beauty blossoms and unites itself to health ; but how many different influences may trouble the soft harmony of these functions! That exquisite tenderness is not always contained in its limits. This little vascular network, so admirable, may be injured in its tenderness and contractibility. The marvellous little organs may be injured in their functions.

Independent of these exterior injuries, the skin presents on its surface a general state of alterations. The complexion loses its brilliancy, the hair is dull, falls, or becomes grey ; the skin alters, wrinkles, and fades. Beauty disappears.

Diseases of the skin are numerous, and their history is so long and odd, that we will

6*

not state them here. Grave alterations of beauty are united with alterations of health. The skin is exposed to so many exterior influences, without being properly called diseases, that are an outrage on beauty, that they should be counteracted if possible. For instance, trembling of the hands results from excitement of the nervous system, and is produced by excess and abuse of alcoholics, moral emotions, passions, fear, anger, etc.

It is sufficient to name them in order, to understand the care and importance one should use, to avoid, if possible, all that tends to excite the nervous system. On this subject I will only add that great attention should be paid to children ; never frighten them. It is an error to believe that at an age when reflection is not developed in a child, that one can punish it, and force it to overcome fear. It is by gentle intervention and coaxing that one can drive away the subject of fear from a child's mind. How many young children, whose nervous system is afflicted by fear, have gone through life and felt its painful influence !

Another deplorable habit among children, and not uncommon among grown persons, is that of scratching themselves before everybody, especially their heads.

It is a habit that can only be overcome by a firm will and hygienic precaution. The first rule consists in avoiding all that tends to excite the nervous system, as generally persons of nervous temperaments are most addicted to this disagreeable habit.

The second consists in avoiding certain food. For instance, all game, pork, cheese, and alcoholic drinks. Sometimes it is absolutely necessary to carefully survey one's habits, and avoid honey, strawberries, almonds, and innumerable other fruits. These precautions should be aided by the greatest cleanliness, constant bathing, lotions, and sometimes tonics; and above all, avoid scratching.

Some persons find it impossible to wear flannel next the skin. I even knew a professor who could only wear female apparel.

Although these afflictions cannot be called diseases, they require hygienic care, with con-

stant bathing. The following mixture is excellent for the baths:

Sub-carbonate of soda...........	1 to 2 drachms.
Distilled Water of Linden........	½ pint.
Essence of Roses............. .	18 grains.

Or a pomade composed of the following:

Chloroform.........................	10 grains.
Fresh Lard........................	1 ounce.
Use for frictions.	

Skin, to be beautiful, should be soft,
smooth, and variable in its polish. It is a
common thing to meet persons whose skin has
not its ordinary softness, but is dull, thick,
and pimpled. This little inconvenience is
generally on the cutaneous surface, but more
prominent on the arms, legs, and thighs,
and at times becomes painful. Persons of
pale complexion suffer most from their skin
in winter. The best remedies for dryness of
the skin are lotions ; such as almond oil, gum-
arabic water, and cocoanut oil. Pomades of
cold cream and glycerine are excellent. The
following is excellent for the lips and face:

A little fresh Butter............ } Equal quantities.
Almond Oil.................... }

ANOTHER.

Fresh Lard......................... 1 ounce.
Peruvian Balm..................... 1 drachm.
Extract of Thebaique.............. 9 grains.
    Mix well, and spread lightly over the face.

ANOTHER.

Cocoanut Butter..................... 1 pound.
White Wax......................... ½ pound.
Spermaceti........................ ½ pound.
    Mix.

There are several diseases of the skin that are natural or hereditary, and although cure is impossible, much can be done to prevent their progress.

Turkish baths are recommended. Sea-bathing is objectionable.

Eruptions on the face result from various causes—change of life, irregular menstruation, and particularly from organic affections and internal diseases, which must be cured before anything can be done for the skin.

Others are the result of accidental or natural causse. Light pimples, sunburn, tan, and freckles always attack fine, delicate skins.

Many persons are affected by a redness in the face, hands, and oftenest in the legs, the result of sitting too near the fire. The use of lotions will aid much to destroy this redness. Pure water with a little lemon-juice often proves an excellent remedy.

Bathe the face in the following lotions:

Sulphate of Zinc..................	9 grains.
Distilled Water.....................	½ pint.
Essence of Lemon...............	10 drops.

Spots on the skin are sometimes large, or small, and deep; they are yellow, brown, or white, and generally arise from an organic affection. Women during pregnancy have them, and in France they are called *masques*.

Sulphur baths are excellent to dispel discolorations of the skin. Generally, tonics are fruitless in these cases.

The use of the following pomade will aid to diminish them:

Subcarbonate of Soda...........	1 to 2 drachms.
Fresh Lard......................	1 ounce.
Essence of Portugal..............	18 grains.

Vinegar and carbonate of soda are both excellent to use in baths.

Discoloration of the skin arises from the absence of the pigment; then it constitutes a general congenital affection, both curious and rare.

Albinism is a complete absence of the coloration. The skin is a milky white; the hair the same, though generally stiff; in many cases it is curly; the eyelashes, etc., the same. *Albinism* is a congenital affection. Albinos are sometimes looked upon as a race among themselves. This is an error. Albinos are found in all the human races. It is plainly seen they can live in almost any climate. It is an organic state which admits of no cure. It is more common among females. In many instances, the hair does not partake of the discoloration, but falls out. With some Albinos, the hair is stiff and jet black, thus making a strange contrast with the face and eyes.

Vitiligo among negroes may be congenital, when it appears in the form of irregular white spots. Negroes affected in this unnatural state are called in French, "*nègres pies,*" or piebald, meaning various colors. This affection of the skin is not really detrimental to beauty, nor is it serious. Various means are used to heighten the color and suspended functions, all more or less exciting in their composition. The best results were from the following pomades :

Aromatic Tincture....................	1 drachm.
Prepared Beef Marrow...............	1 ounce.
Carefully mix.	

ANOTHER.

Tannin...........................	1 drachm.
Fresh Lard.......................	1 ounce.
Tincture of Cinnamon..............	18 grains.
Mix, and wash the discolored spots.	

A little lukewarm water and salt is a soothing lotion. Friction has a good effect. Sulphur baths are also highly recommended.

There is another alteration of the skin in various forms and colors, which is congenital and incurable. These spots are designated under the name of spili (de σπιλος, macule), but commonly called and known as *envies* or "longing marks," attributed to certain impressions received by mothers during pregnancy. Those spots are not confined to the face alone, but may be on any part of the body, though generally on the neck and hands. Their surface is smooth, and their shape irregular; the color varies. Sometimes they are yellow, and are called "*taches de café,*" or coffee-stains; when red, "wine spots;" when black, they are generally covered with short, thick hairs.

Frequently, when examining the nape of the neck and the scalp, I was struck in seeing how common it was to find among women little irregular red spots at the roots of the hair, covering a part of the neck. I have known cases where they have been mistaken for skin diseases. I have also seen, though not so frequently, an analogical redness of the eyelids, in an irregular form, sometimes extending down the side of the face. This is considered congenital; although it is unperceived in early youth, it is more plainly seen in later years.

Birth-marks are indeed injurious to
beauty. It is very difficult, if not impossible, to cure them. At most, we may hope
to diminish them by the use of astringent
lotions, at the same time using internal means
to avoid the tendency to congestion of the
face.

For the red spots at the roots of the hair
and the nape of the neck, there is nothing to
be done. Fortunately, they occupy an invisible place, as they are covered by the
hair ; therefore are of so little importance,
that many are unaware of them. The dark
spots might be removed by cauterizing, but
one risks making an indelible scar which
would be unsightlier than the spots themselves. If they are very small, they may be
hidden by a little cold cream and powder.

The skin is affected by another species of
spots, which are congenital tumors, and do
not alter the skin, but the veins. The veins,
when altered, are called *nævi vasculaires.*
They are sometimes superficial and excessively variable. Their red color will often
change by a momentary pressure of the

hand. They remain only a short time, and require very little care. These are more frequent among persons of light complexion. Constipation is one cause of these little eruptions. Much caution must be used in choice of curatives. Among the means most recommended, are the following :

VIENNA WATER.

Almond Bran........... 1 ounce and 7 drachms.
Orange-flower Water............... ½ pint.
Rose-water....................... ¼ pint.
    Make a mixture, and add
Borax............................ 1 drachm.
Tincture of Benzoin.............:. 2 drachms.
    Mix.

VIRGIN MILK.

Tincture of Benzoin................ 1 drachm.
Rose-water....................... 1 pint.
    Mix carefully.

With age, beauty fades gradually. The capillary circulation is less active, the cutaneous sensibility becomes weakened, the cellulary tissues collapse ; the skin is no longer sustained, so it flags, and folds itself into furrows called wrinkles.

We cannot escape the ravages of time. These ravages are often favored by incidental conditions; a sanguine temperament is less disposed than a bilious one. In general, stout persons become wrinkled late in life. Is it because obesity seems to exclude the influence of the passions and emotions which, on the contrary, are frequently the appanage of bilious temperaments, and which explains the vulgar diction: "*Grosses gens bonnes gens*"?

However, many persons have wrinkles that are not caused by age, and are visible everywhere; but those most injurious to beauty are seen on the face, neck, cheeks, and hands. Aristotle said that precocious wrinkles proved a man effeminate, soft, and timid. This assertion is far from true. There are certainly wrinkles in adults, and even in youths, generally appearing after serious illness, or when persons who have been fleshy become thin. They are also the result of excessive grief and labor, late hours, and contentions of the mind.

It is as difficult to banish accidental wrinkles as those that accompany old age; however, we may see those disappear that result from grave maladies or a passing decrease in flesh.

Nevertheless, various means are proposed to dispel accidental wrinkles; such as frictions with almond oil, fresh lard, fresh butter, and alumine lotions :

Sulphate of Alumine......... 1 scruple, 16 grains.
Pure Water.......................... ½ pint.
Mix, and bathe the face three times a day.

POMADE.

Essence of Turpentine............... 2 drachms.
Mastic .... 1 drachm.
Fresh Butter .... 2 drachms.
Mix, and anoint the face.

In the most remote ages women used lotions with sublimate. The best formula for it is the following :

Sublimate........................... 4 grains.
Hydrochlorate of Ammonia .... 4 grains.
Milk of Almonds (a little thick)........ ½ pint.
Mix carefully.

If they cannot be dispelled, they may be palliated by various means. For a long time paint has been used. Ovid said, in his work called "The Art of Love," "*Vous empruntez à la ceruse sa blancheur trompeuse.*"

In spite of the criticism of which paint has been the object, in spite of the accidents which the voice of caution has warned against it, the use of white lead is still employed under different names, as *blanc de perle*, blanc d'argent, etc. It is preferred because it adheres to the skin ; and yet it is not only a grave injury, but has the disadvantage of altering and wrinkling the skin.

It has been replaced to a certain extent by the use of bismuth chalk prepared as powder or pomade.

VEGETABLE ROUGE.

Cetaceum	1 pound.
Carthamine Rouge...................	3 drachms.
Spermaceti........................	2 ounces.

Pound all together, add a little pure water. Let it dry.

These cosmetics are without the least danger. It is well to use a little pulverized starch when applying the rouge with a rabbit's or hare's foot, which can always be purchased at a druggist's. Some persons prefer to apply the rouge with a little glycerine or cold cream.

Nothing so defaces beauty of the skin as scars on the face. These indelible traces of ancient sores or wounds, unfortunately more or less apparent, never disappear.

The long duration of scars is quite historical. It was noted in the remote ages of antiquity. Ulysses, after his long voyages and misfortunes, was not recognized by his friends, nor even by his nurse, until she saw the scar he had on his knee.

Scars are variable according to the causes which produce them. They constitute an infirmity more or less painful, according to their extent in form.

Sometimes scars only alter the surface of the skin ; and again they multiply on the surface, and change to a deformed aspect the expression of the face, like small-pox.

Scars caused by burns leave marks of (sometimes) little importance, yet superficial in color ; but with time they change, and resemble the natural color of the skin. Scars received in youth often disappear with age and growth. I have seen various cases of children who were badly burned, but when developed, the scars were scarcely visible.

Certainly there are scars so bad and enormous that all art is powerless.

Pliny tells us that mandrake served to remove scars from the face. And, according to Ovid, poppies were employed for the same purpose. In the present age, these plants have lost that pleasing effect. Scars, like wrinkles, and perhaps more so, must be wisely accepted, or else covered.

So what I have said of paints and powders is quite applicable to them.

CREAM FOR WRINKLES.

White Wax...................... 1 drachm.
Cetaceum........................ 1 drachm.
  Melt in a water bath, and add—
Rose-water...................... 2 drachms.
Tincture of Balm of Tolu.. 1 scruple, 16 grains.
  Mix, and anoint the face.

ANOTHER.

Alcohol......................... 4 drachms.
White of Eggs................... 4 drachms.

Pastes of powdered starch, and of oil of cochineal, I have seen so perfectly made as

to imitate the color of the skin. The difficulty is to prevent them from melting or becoming detached under the influence of perspiration. On one occasion I saw a Polish
lady whose nose had been cauterized at
Vienna, and which had at its extremity a
frightful scar, surrounded with little holes
that gave it the appearance of a skimmer.

. She was beautiful and graceful, and one
can well imagine this disfigurement grieved
her. She tried various means to conceal it,
and with admirable patience made a paste so
artfully combined, that it was exactly the
color of the skin, and with the aid of a little anatomical instrument she filled the holes
and covered them with a last coating ; when
finished, no one (unless they were very close)
could tell the difference. Unfortunately, it
would not last long. The heat, perspiration,
and a thousand exterior causes, compelled
this frail mask to succumb. She used it
particularly when going out, but her visits
had to be short, as her mask did not remain
intact more than two or three hours. She
did all she could while in Paris to obtain

7

some means of preserving it for twenty-four hours, but she failed.

For certain scars it is well to try tattooing, but with the greatest precaution in regard to the substance employed, for one risks incurring a disfigurement still more disagreeable.

PERSPIRATION.

THE skin throughout exhales a vapor which does not escape our senses, and appears in a liquid form.

Visible or insensible perspiration, which escapes from the body, is a very disagreeable fluid. The celebrated Mercuriali said: "Beauty is principally found in a good physical condition calculated to flatter the sense of view; yet if a disagreeable odor issue from the body, it must be called a vice of beauty." The skin sometimes exhales a particular odor, arising from certain food and drinks; from eating onions, rabbits, truffles, and cabbage.

Every one has a special odor. Certain races, particularly the negroes, the Esquimaux, and the Terra del Fuego races, have a most disgusting smell, resulting from their habits and manner of living. Their quality of food is generally greasy, and they eat large quantities of bad fish. As I have already remarked, every individual has his or her particular smell. It varies according to age and sex, particularly among women. It is influenced by special circumstances ; as moral emotions, passion, anger, will in one moment change the odor that characterizes habitual health.

But, unfortunately, with certain individuals whose hygienic conditions are perfect, and whose habits of cleanliness are minute, the odor is often most disagreeable, especially disgusting with red-haired persons and blondes.

Although this excretion is useful to those who are fleshy and in good health, it is in itself an inconvenience when too abundant. I do not wish to enter into medical detail on the different kinds of perspiration, such as

red, blue, and black ; I leave that subject to
medical authors.   Periodical perspirations
are simply stages of intermittent fevers, that
disappear by careful treatment, and by administering quinine.   Sometimes they are
confined to certain parts of the body : the
armpits, the palms of the hands, the feet,
and sometimes the scalp, and often the
breasts ; but when the odors are disagreeable,
they mostly arise from the armpits.

Perspiration may be habitual and general.
It is well known that some persons perspire
from the least exercise ; a short walk, or the
slightest fatigue, will cause it ; and with some
persons it is so habitual and abundant it
renders them infirm.   I have seen many examples, and one especially remarkable—a
bishop, a highly educated man, most amiable
in disposition, industrious, and active.   The
slightest fatigue and ordinary conversation
caused him to perspire.   This affection poi-
soned his very life.

If he wished to write a moment, he was
teeming with perspiration.   At the slightest
change in the temperature he had a cold in

his head, and when cured, the sweat would return as before; thus he passed his life, taking cold and getting rid of it.

The causes of perspiration are many. It is often an organic and hereditary disposition. Heat, warm drinks, and aromatics are natural causes. Dupont tells of a rare and curious exception, that "Some who had a copious perspiration in summer, were troubled in the same way in winter." "*Qui dormuit magis sudant.*"

Moral emotions, shame, fear, terror, and grief, are powerful causes. In a medicinal point of view, it is not easy to remedy the excess of this secretion, notwithstanding all means have been employed with circumspect prudence. It is very easy to say what one must avoid; abstaining from warm drinks and taking cooling ones during perspiration, have caused fatal accidents. The same in bathing. Great care should be taken to have the body free from heat, and the skin as dry as possible. One can use to great advantage tepid baths, and render them tonic by a little "rock salt," or hydrosulphate of potash.

Strengthening food, such as broths, roast meats, wine, and coffee, elixir of Peruvian bark, frequent changes of the underclothing, wearing flannel next the skin, not covering the body too much, and avoiding sudden drafts : this is the most important advice one can offer, although we suggest, independent of this, means of assuaging the odor, arising from the excess of perspiration.

To those who suffer profusely at the armpits, wipe them night and morning with a fine piece of flannel, and when retiring, wash with rose-water, or lemon and water. To have the underclothing perfumed is also an excellent thing—Mercuriali says, by a "little musk," or "amber wood;" this we do not approve of, but think it is only adding one disagreeable odor to another ; and thus we differ with this celebrated author. We do not condemn perfumes less diffusible than musk, for they might prove agreeable if employed in a small quantity.

For the feet, bathe them three times a week

one hour, in a decoction of ashes, steeped laurel leaves, and a little turpentine.

As to the diet, it is well to exclude such substances as fish, cheese, etc.

The following lotion is an excellent aromatic :

Essence of Mint............ ⎫
Essence of Lavender........ ⎬ Of each, 2 scruples.
Essence of Rosemary........ ⎮
Essence of Lemon .... ⎭
Alcohol......................... 1½ ounce.
Infusion of Thyme................. 1 quart.
    Mix.

POWDER.

Cinnamon .... ⎫
Pulverized Starch .... ⎬ Equal parts.
Cardamom .... ⎭
    Mix.

Perfumed baths are highly recommended, but are exceedingly expensive. The following, however, is an excellent prescription :

    Aromatic Plant.
    Boiling Water.
    Eau de Cologne, or,
    Alcohol.
       Pour the whole in the bath.

CHAPTER IV.

OBESITY.

THE mass of fat in the cellular tissue beneath the skin, and in the interstices of the adjoining muscles, when contained in certain limits, is detrimental to beauty. It spoils the form when excessive, and annoys the functions and movements of the body. The annals of science contain a number of cases on this subject. In a work entitled, "Philosophic Transactions," are found examples of men who weighed five hundred to five hundred and eighty-four pounds. Franck cites numerous cases from different authors, particularly Beclard, who tells us of a boy, four years and a half old, who weighed one hundred pounds; and

Tartra, of a certain Lambert, aged forty, who died at London, in eighteen hundred and nine (1809), and who weighed 739 pounds. However this may be under the influence of fat, the body becomes soft, clammy, and the muscles invisible, the liberty and force of movement lost. After eating, a need of sleep is felt ; the least movement causes perspiration and painful oppression. Obesity is sometimes partial. It is common with women ; with men it is generally observed in the abdomen.

This infirmity is often hereditary. Sometimes, if not congenital, it commences soon after birth, and with infants it sometimes reaches wonderful development. United frequently to a lymphatic temperament, it only awaits a concourse of favorable circumstances to develop itself. The circumstances are : sedentary life, habits of laziness, prolonged sleep, physical and moral inaction.

Prosper Alpin has remarked, that in Egypt the régimen of the inhabitants, the abuse of certain pleasures, the habitual use of warm baths, and the sultry climate, made the men

7*

extremely corpulent. Nevertheless, cold climates also produce the same influence.

Larry attributes an extreme influence to moral emotions. On the other side, Franck cites a curious case—the extraordinary obesity of a new-born infant on account of a sudden emotion of the mother. The greatest influence on the development of obesity, after a lymphatic temperament, is the food. It is observed among high livers and those that are accustomed to nutritious food. Another thing to be remarked : those employed in certain trades and professions—for instance, the butchers—are invariably fat. Fat originates often from constant use of certain food, as bread, butter, milk, sugar, beer, potatoes and spirits ; assist its development, if not produce it, particularly at a certain period of life.

The use of fruits, dates, sweetened drinks also increase and encourage it. With some persons, the excess of flesh, instead of making them ugly, renders them really fine. There is a something united to a sanguine temperament, that the increase of flesh, united to high color, renders attractive. It is, however, a great inconvenience, and in all times has claimed the attention of physicians. In any case, it is far from being considered beautiful with us. A host of means are praised to reduce corpulency, which are not commendable. However, it is not impossible to diminish it, if strict attention is paid to hygienic rules. Seek a warm, dry air, the action of fire, sunshine, sleep on a hard bed, lead an active life, practise intellectual labors; regular exercises, fencing, gymnastics, and dancing, are very efficacious; plain food, and not too abundant; no sweetmeats, little bread, and acid drinks in large quantities. To these hygienic means may be added with advantage, friction, alkaline baths, salt-water baths, and above all, vapor baths, aided by shampooing. I obtained excellent relief by administering iodine internally, and also by passing a season at the waters of Kreuznach. Banting's treatment has long been highly praised, and has cured many difficult cases of corpulency. The following are his statements : "At the age of sixty-six I weighed 202 pounds ; in less than twenty days I lost 46. At breakfast, four or five ounces of beef or mutton, broiled fish, cold meat of all sorts except fresh pork, a cup of tea without milk or sugar, a little biscuit, or an ounce of toasted bread. At dinner, five or six ounces of fish (not salmon) or meat (not fresh pork), all kinds of vegetables (not potatoes), an ounce of toasted bread, a little fruit, no pastry, no poultry or game; two or three wine glasses of good Bordeaux or Madeira (champagne, Port wine, and beer prohibited at tea) ; two or three ounces of fruit, a cup of tea without milk or sugar.

"At supper, three or four ounces of meat or fish ; as at dinner, one or two glasses of Bordeaux. Before retiring, if one feels the need, a glass of Bordeaux or Xèrès."

Such is Banting's treatment.

Of course it may be modified according to the habits or health of the individual. The English customs differ from ours. However, the important point is in the regularity and composition. As to the danger, I do not believe in any. I have known persons follow it up with good effects.

Mr. Banting advises those who follow the treatment to get weighed before commencing, and re-weighed each succeeding week; he gives a table indicating the weight that should generally accompany a certain stature.

SIZE.	WEIGHT.
5 feet 1	120 pounds.
5 " 2	126 "
5 " 3	133 "
5 " 4	136 "
5 " 5	142 "
5 " 6	145 "
5 " 7	148 "
5 " 8	155 "
5 " 9	162 "
5 " 10	169 "
5 " 11	174 "
6 "	178 "

LEANNESS.

HERE are a great many persons who are so fat they long to be lean—but there are a greater number who are so lean they wish to be fat. However, leanness is no indication of a bad constitution. Many lovely women grieve over their leanness, and often do the most useless things to recover flesh; they forget how light, graceful, and easy they are in their movements. Meagreness is general or partial; with women it is in the breast, and with men in the legs. I am only speaking of constitutional or accidental meagreness, which is no symptom of ill-health. Contrary to obesity, it belongs to a nervous, bilious temperament. Thin people are in general lively, excitable, easily agitated, and sometimes of an extreme susceptibility. They sleep but little, have a good appetite; yet with all that they enjoy excellent health. For a temperament disposed to leanness, a host of causes may produce it—warm climates, abstinences, irregularity of meals, excessive bodily labor, and still more, intellectual labor, late hours, abuse of pleasures, and contentions of the mind. Lorry said grief was the principal cause of it. Envious, nervous, restless, melancholy, and ambitious persons are rarely fat like those who take things easy. Nothing is more capable of producing meagreness than a mad love, and worst of all, jealousy. This last passion has been signalized in all ages, even outside of love. Andry reminds us that it exists among children, and reduces them to such an extent as to make them fretful and peevish without the parents ever discovering it. Children often become jealous when nursing, if they see a brother or sister petted or caressed.

St. Augustine in his celebrated confession says: "I have seen a jealous infant too young to utter a word, his little eyes flashing with anger, and his face pale with vexation, while seeing another nursing with him."

It is common to see young people grow thin without any apparent cause other than a hereditary disposition, but as they advance in life grow fleshy.

The means to prevent meagreness consist simply in a regular life, moderation in pleasures, moderate exercise, certain hours of labor, never excessive ; avoid as much as possible all that may excite the nervous system ; reasonable hours of rest, and if possible, in the midst of all the agitations of life, seek tranquillity of soul and contentment of mind.

Abundant nutritious food is also recommended, yet one sees daily thin persons who have excellent appetites and eat an abundance of animal and vegetable food, without ever growing stout. The use of meat and vegetables, combined, moderate drinks, such as pure wine and beer, will aid and increase flesh. Pure milk taken every morning is excellent. Baths, simple and emollient, should also be used.

CHAPTER V.

BEAUTY—Resumed.

AVING examined in detail the conditions that contribute to beauty, there are still a few general considerations to add.

"Question the soul in presence of beauty," said Cousin. Is it not an incontestable fact that in presence of certain objects and divers circumstances we carry this judgment: That object is beautiful. With us it is a widespread opinion that the sentiment and idea of beauty are things purely arbitrary and individual. For those who reason thus the *beautiful* confounds itself with the *agreeable*, but all things agreeable do not appear beau-

tiful; and among the former that which is
most agreeable is farthest from beautiful.

While all our senses give us agreeable sensations, two alone have the privilege of
awakening .in us the idea of beauty. No
one ever said, "What a beautiful flavor!"
"What a beautiful odor!" The sentiment
of the beautiful is a special one; like the
idea of the beautiful, it is *sui generis*. The
idea of the beautiful is the idea of the true
manifested under a sensible form. Plato has
admirably said: "The beautiful is the splendor of the true." Physical beauty is purely
exterior, yet beautiful to contemplate, considered, as it is, a reflection of the moral.
I should, however, speak particularly of
woman.

"The fair sex," said Bernardin de Saint
Pierre, "is particularly for those who have
eyes alone. It is also for those who have a
heart. It is the generating sex, who carry
man in their womb for nine months at the
peril of their lives; the cherishing sex, who
nourish and care for infancy; the pious sex,
that takes him to the altar; the pacific sex,

who do not spill the blood of their fellow-creatures; the consoling sex, who care for the sick without wounding them. If woman has certain qualities that essentially belong to her in all climates, in all ranks of society, in all ages of civilization, there are among others those that touch the beautiful, which need to be favored by force of cultivation and care. Thus delicacy, gentleness, the bend of the form, the lightness of movement, the grace and flexibility of attitude, the elasticity and fineness of the skin, the fascinating traits of the visage, can only be developed in the first ages of social life. They were blasted at their birth by persecutions, slavery, violent exercise, and continual exposure to inclement atmospheres.

That beauty of whose existence savages had no idea, only needed for its development social art to ameliorate the condition of woman; and to-day what a difference exists! What charms are visible in the inferior ranks of society! Yet often, on account of vicious habits, excessive labor under the influence of misery and debauchery, the traits have lost their fineness, the attitude becomes coarse, and the expression of the visage blighted. Beauty once flown can never return. Women have a far more lively physiognomy than men. Their sentiments are more movable ; they have far more mobility in their features. Apart from that mobility, there is in the delicacy of their muscles, the softness of their skin, the contour of their visage, something that removes the strongly accentuated features that characterize man. Advancing in life, they lose that softness and freshness, but gain in physiognomy and expression what they have lost in beauty. This explains the particular charms that mature and even old age often leaves on the face of woman :

> Moins jeune encore la beauté nous engage,
> L'art du maintien, les grâces du langage,
> Les dons acquis, les charmes empruntés,
> Donnent un lustre au couchant des beautés,
> L'amour, fidèle à leurs flammes constantes,
> Se glisse encore, sous des rides naissantes,
> Et pour regner jusqu'aux derniers instants,
> Sème de fleurs les ruines du temps.—BERNARD.

Many differ as to real beauty, yet with few exceptions it has been celebrated and praised in all ages. Zeuxis, who was requested to paint the portrait of Helen, who passed for a perfect beauty, contemplated several beautiful women, and chose from each one that which he found most remarkable. In a work written by Jean Nevisan, entitled "Beauty and Merit of Women," thirty qualities are requisite to be a perfect beauty. Francis Corniger wrote them in Latin, and Brantôme translated them into French. I cite a few lines and leave the rest to the imagination :

" Three things white—the skin, the teeth, and hands.
  Three black—the eyes, the eyebrows, and lashes.
  Three red—the lips, cheeks, and nails.
  Three long—the body, the hair, and hands.
  Three short—the teeth, the ears, and feet.
  Three large—the bust, the head, and brow."

    .   .   .   .

Among the multitude of works written in honor of women during the revival of literature in Europe, a great number are naturally dedicated to their charms and beauty. Moralists, philosophers, and metaphysicians occupied themselves with the subject; they are said to have made it superficial, and at times pretentious. Ninon, reproaching them in an interview with Bernier, said, "The philosophers have not studied us seriously; we have been for them as for our lovers, the object of a light fancy, rather than a serious study."

But the natural history of woman, and the analysis of beauty, have been the objects of a serious study by many scholars, physiologists, and physicians (I speak of modern times only), among whom were Thomas and Roussel, who in his work, "Moral and Physical System of Woman," enriched his details with grace, sentiment, and charm purely scientific. Also the remarkable work of Moreau de La Saithe, "Natural History of Woman," from which I borrow the remarks also on his notes of Lavater's Treatise. Another remarkable work on beauty was written by Andry. Beauty, however, has not escaped detraction, be it from an almost criminal exaggeration of puritanism, or like

the two mothers of whom Andry speaks in his
"Orthopédie" from a religious exaggeration
cruel in the extreme. Parents, said Andry,
are not all like that odd mother, who seeing
.her daughter's teeth were too beautiful, and
fearing they would make her vain, had them
all drawn out. Or like another cruel mother,
who caused her child—who was beautifully
formed—to continually stoop, so as not to
attract worldly praise. Réné François, in
a long debate against beauty, says, "What
is all that which is called beauty? Two bits
of broken glass encased in two little hollows
covered with a little leather flounce, bordered
with little threads; these are called 'eyes.'
An ivory table slightly arched, covered with
a satin skin without a wrinkle; a little snow
mixed with scarlet makes the cheeks, neither
too full nor too hollow; between the two is
the canal that unites all grace. A little piece
of bloody flesh cut in two makes the lips. I
know not how many ossicles attached to the
caked blood and rooted in the flesh make
the gums. A flat piece of flesh inside, quite
movable, allows the air to pass and facili-

tates our muttering; the whole surrounded with a large wig. Is not there a subject for a grand clatter?" No one will doubt that it is proper to care for and preserve the grace and beauty of the human form. Nay! it is even a duty. The first means should be devoted to health. Health, as well as beauty, may be the object of exaggerated care. Few think seriously of it until it is altered. Beauty cannot exist without the means that preserve the harmony of our organs and the freedom of our functions. It requires particular care, and that care is cosmetic.

Cosmetic, taken in the general acceptation of the word, has an importance that is worthy of marked attention. It is the art with which the ancients decorated the name of science, (scientia cosmetica Mercuriali), and belongs to medicine by its hygienic precepts.

CHAPTER VI.

COSMETICS.

HYGIENE—PERFUMES—COSMETICS.

COSMETIC, like antiquity, constitutes an art from which results all practical means employed in human decoration. With the ancients it formed a branch of medicine in turn honored and reproached. It reached us in the middle of the most incredible abuse and exaggerated criticisms. It constitutes, I repeat, an art that requires a precise and serious examination so as to end the ridiculous pretensions and attacks of which it has been the object, and which are often unjust. The Greeks—passionate admirers of beauty—professed a great

8

veneration for those who cultivated it. Aspasia and Cleopatra wrote a complete treatise on cosmetic. Pliny and Ovid have also transmitted to us numerous formulas. The habits of the Roman dames were for a long time very severe under the Republic. During several centuries, their dress and appearance was modest and simple. The use of silk and linen was not introduced until the time of the Cæsars.

Under the Emperors it is said the women seemed to forget that their clothing should cover them. The courtesans were the first who dared to adopt new fashions; then all the ladies imitated them. The progress of corruption is the same at all times. Soon the Roman ladies carried the art of cosmetics to extremes. All the details of the toilette, the hair, teeth, softness of the skin, etc., were the object of particular care. Paint supplanted color, and they wore false hair, etc. They had a sort of mask designed to cover the face when at home. Juvenal said, "It was the domestic face offered to their husbands." In the midst of the ostentatious luxury which reigned under the Roman emperors, cosmetics became a regular industry.

Seneca reproached the Roman dames for the time passed in keeping their beauty in such refined elegance and luxury. Clement of Alexandria assures us that the most elegant women pass the day between the comb and glass. True it is that cosmetic comes from and is borne everywhere, especially with woman, who knows she should charm and please.

In spite of the invasion of the barbarians, the domination of the French over Gaul, the cultivation of beauty never lost its empire. When the Arabs conquered Spain, they introduced the use of perfumery and cosmetics.

Later, at the return of the Templars to the court of love, they discussed gallantry and beauty.

Albert the Great then wrote his famous "Book of Secrets," etc., which was translated into French two centuries after, and printed in 1440. The *Renaissance* was a glorious time for cosmetics. Grace to the secrets given by Paracelsus! Diana of Poitiers preserved all her charms when she had far passed the age of pleasing. The secret, it is said, consisted in using a rain-water bath every morning.

During that time, the secrets of Italian cosmetics met with great success, and many valuable books were written on the art; one by the celebrated Marinello, called "The Ornaments of Woman." Later, Italian cosmetics and perfumery lost much when introduced by Francis I., and Catherine de Medicis. Neglected under Henry IV., it appeared again at the elegant court of Louis XIII., in all its luxury and *éclat.*

Louis XIV. detested perfumes and cosmetics; so, for the second time, it completely disappeared from his court, to reappear under the regency, and to cosmetic is attributed the charms of the women that were so beautiful at that time. Again it reached an exaggerated use, but became more simple under the delicate taste and influence of Marie Antoinette, and in spite of the extravagances of the

Directory, it still retains the same condition. It passed the Revolution of 1789, and reached the most curious exaggeration, such as "Dress à la guillotine," "Pomade of Sanson," etc. ; in short, all the abuses that existed in Greece and Rome appeared in an instant. The ladies revived the perfumed baths, and Madame Tallien, stepping from a strawberry and raspberry bath, was gently rubbed with a sponge dipped in milk and perfumes. Nevertheless, if the use of cosmetic is generally coupled with habits of luxury, and has pushed to excess the use of paints, ridiculous fashions have almost disappeared. Women are no longer the martyrs of fashion, but, alas! many continue to exaggerate at the expense of elegance and simplicity. At the present day, however, cosmetic holds an independent code in the toilette, as well as a serious and scientific rank in the hygiene of beauty.

It is an absurdity, said Celsus, to take care of warts, spots, and freckles. Nevertheless, there is no use in trying to prevent women from taking care of their beauty.

Franck said, "The art of cosmetic consisted in a great measure in the means of preserving and increasing the sincerity of beauty, and these means, united to health, demanded of prophylactic medicine incontestable right and attention."

Cosmetic considered, in short, in all the extent of its object—that is to say, cultivation of beauty—is far from limiting itself to the practice of perfumes more or less numerous. It should extend and apply itself to a multitude of hygienic rules, and from them take the principal means of preserving and combating the influences that tend to destroy it. Cosmetics are the accessory means generally designed to complete and repair the damage that beauty may receive.

CHAPTER VII.

HYGIENE.

THE first rule of hygiene is cleanliness. Ablutions have been recommended at all times; they have even been made a religious precept. Moses and Mohammed recommended ablutions of cold water; and at the present day a good Mussulman says five prayers and makes five ablutions daily.

Pure cold water is the best medium for cleanliness. It is necessary, sometimes, to second its action by adding soap or a little eau de cologne. For the face, use cold water; for the hands or feet, use warm or lukewarm. The ablutions for the toilet should be warm in winter, fresh, but never cold, in summer. For several years the use of ablutions of water from eight to twelve degrees has been a custom. Lukewarm water is best for the beauty of the skin.

Sponge baths are excellent. Shower-baths are also commendable, but great care should be taken afterwards to dry the body quickly, and walk rapidly for at least fifteen minutes. In whatever manner baths are used, wiping the skin perfectly dry is very important.

Baths are a natural usage, established from the most remote antiquity, and are to be found among the least civilized savages. The woollen clothing worn by the ancients rendered the practice of bathing necessary at all times. In fact, it was an essentially hygienic use with them. The Persians and the Egyptians were the first peoples among whom were found vestiges of this ancient custom.

The Romans did not build their baths till towards the end of the Republic; but during the reign of the emperors the luxury of these establishments increased to such a point, that at the present day the baths of Caracalla, Diocletian, Agrippa, and Augustus are the admiration of all travellers through Italy ; and traces of that splendor are still found in several thermal establishments in France, Germany, and Algeria. Cold baths of from twelve to fifteen degrees are bad for the skin. A bath, for cleanliness, should · be from twenty to twenty-five degrees, and it softens and tones the skin. A river bath has the same effect.

Rain-water is the best water for bathing, after river-water. Nevertheless, water may be artificially changed, according to the purpose for which it is used—as, to render it emollient and soften the skin, favor the movements, etc. . . . We have already recommended various soaps and aromatics for the toilet.

Vapor-baths have at all times been a luxurious pleasure among the Turks, Egyptians, and Persians. With the Indians and Turks they contain various perfumes and delicate aromatics ; joined to these, frictions of the most fragrant oils and essences; while shampooing is done by the most skilful hands. Sorbets, coffee, and tobacco are absolutely necessary to this *genre* of pastime. With us

8*

the Russian bath is composed of vapor, followed by affusions and showers of cold water, friction, and sudation, which is obtained by lying on a bed, wrapped in blankets.

For the skin, a simple vapor-bath—that is to say, without a shower—is best, unless the water is warm. It is better to walk than repose afterwards.

As to hydropathy, that consists in the employment of cold water, in different ways, to provoke sudation. It is injurious to beauty, and bad for the skin.

Among those that are praised for soothing the skin and refining the toilet of ladies, I would particularly recommend an oil or milk bath, and also the ancient custom of anointing the body after the bath with perfumed oil or essence. This use still exists, particularly among the Orientals. The Egyptians cover themselves from head to foot with lather, perfume their hair with essence of rose, and rub their feet with pumice-stone, in order to make them hard. This practice may prove beneficial for softening the skin and removing its dryness. A simple vapor-bath, with or without shampooing, is useful and necessary.

Day is to labor ; night, to rest and renovate our strength. It is important to arrange the hours of labor according to one's strength. It is a great disadvantage to make day of night ; those who are obliged to do so, end by having weak, sunken eyes, and a pale, faded expression. In all intellectual labors, there should be certain rules.

Abuse of balls, theatres, etc., is very injurious.

Although sleep is called the best part of our lives, it is a bad habit to sleep too much. It tends to produce corpulency. It is easy to know what measures to adopt, according to age, sex, and temperament.

I might add as much concerning diet, but need not here speak of its quality, having already noted the results of certain food for certain persons, etc. I have already objected to alcoholic drinks.

The quantity of food should be in proportion with age, exercise, etc. Men generally eat too much, and often irregularly.

Business fever, united to that of exciting pleasures, has much to do with irregular meals.

Sobriety is health ; without health there is no true beauty.

If it appear absurd not to eat a sufficiency of food, it is good sense not to give the stomach all it craves. It is an old truth that one should always "leave the table with room for more."

Regular meals (without eating between them), and moderate exercise after, is a simple rule.

Supper, that favorite repast of our fathers, should be universally abolished. Monsieur Beaugrand reminds one of this subject in an ancient diction of the fifteenth century :

> " Lever à cinq, dîner à neuf,
>   Souper à cinq, coucher à neuf,
>   Fait vivre d'ans nonante et neuf."

Muscular exercise is conducive to health and consequently to beauty. It keeps the body in an energetic state, favors circulation, and in a word contributes to the physical development and perfection of form. This activity, however, should be limited.

Swimming is a pleasing exercise, because its movement are regular, and assist the development of the chest. Fencing is an excellent exercise ; it favors the development of the chest, and gives to man nobility and grace.

Dancing is also a natural exercise. Even in the most remote ages, and among savages, it was a favorite one. But I am now, be it understood, alluding to the dance of thirty years since, and not to the slow, stamping movement in the middle of a crowd, where attitude or space is an impossibility at the present day. I allude particularly to dancing in the open air, because in small *salons*, in the midst of a crowd, the air is warm, impure ; therefore it is certainly detrimental to health. Rushing from the heat of a dance to cold air, has sent many a one to an early grave.

Gymnastics is one of the important branches of early education.

In ancient Greece, it was one of three distinct branches, comprised in the education of youth, and one to which they attached great importance.

The Greeks owed to that passion for gymnastics the perfection of form and admirable proportion that distinguished them from all other people.

Colonel Amoros founded gymnastics in France. The choice of gymnastics is important for the end that one wishes to attain, but in general they are salutary for the development of physical beauty.

Walking is the simplest and most natural of exercises, as it necessitates alternate movements of the legs and feet. One may even walk lazily along, and yet succeed in accelerating circulation, and give an agreeable warmth to the skin.

Swinging and riding are highly praised.

Equestrianism has two advantages; which are, preventing excessive stoutness, and favoring grace of figure.

Man, deprived of natural means of protection against the inclemency of the weather, supplies the deficiency by means of clothing. The Greeks and Romans went habitually bareheaded. This custom has a few disadvantages : it favors wrinkles on the forehead, and around the eyes. The head should always be covered in the open air. Many people are opposed to sleeping in nightcaps. It is a point that admits of no discussion, and has little advantage for beauty. Children should be dressed in a manner appropriate to the season and climate. It is a deplorable custom to let children go out with bare necks, bare arms, and bare legs. Nothing is so fatal to beauty as to pass from a cold to a warm air, because it is injurious to the skin.

Women generally have their necks and throats uncovered. It is an excellent habit. It is well, however, to cover them with some light garment. It is not so with the breast, so frequently exposed to the vicissitudes of a cold air. Remarkable to state, English ladies pass for the most prudish women in Europe, and yet in no place has the fashion of low necks and bare arms made such progress as in England.

Ladies' clothing is often contrary to hygiene; head-dresses and bonnets are more ornamental than useful. One good thing, however, is the veil, because it protects the face from the cold wind in winter, and dust and sunburn in summer. Gloves are also excellent, especially kid gloves, because they protect the hands from the cold, as well as preserve and soften the skin.

For a century, physicians and philosophers have occupied themselves with the advantage and disadvantage of corsets. Buffon and Rousseau declared legitimate war against those whalebone waist-boards that deformed and pressed the waists of our grandmothers. Thank God, they are no longer worn.

The Greek and Roman ladies, contrary to the opinion of Rousseau, laced and strapped their waists so much, that the satiric authors of the time made fun of them. That custom disappeared in modern times. Under Henry II., in the middle of the sixteenth century, whalebone corsets were worn, which imprisoned the breast in a painful manner. Since the Revolution, corsets have been modified, and are the same as under Catherine de Medicis. But as it is, when laced tight, especially on young persons, they deform the waist, press, and impede the growth of the breasts. Bouvier said, "Corsets should never be stiff," nor tightened across the breast; the whalebones should be thin and flexible, with ample room on the side for the hips. Young girls should not wear corsets before the age of puberty, unless they are delicate, and tend to stoop. Physicians say corsets should not be worn until the form is completely developed. In spite of the changes made in corsets, in spite of the numerous warnings given concerning them, hundreds of women continue to lace and press their waists, at the price of internal suffering and weakness.

Even the form of the shoe has varied in all times and among all peoples. The Hebrews only wore shoes in the country. The Romans had two kinds of shoes, *sandals* and *calceus*, that completely covered their feet and resembled our half-boots.

Men wore black ones, and women generally white, sometimes red bound or embellished with pearls.

Henry IV. rode horseback so much, that he wore boots, and then all the captains followed him.

Louis XIII. wore his boots Spanish fashion, tight fit, high, large, and the tops falling over below the knee.

During the reign of Louis XVI. and in 1789, the boots that were discarded under Louis XIV. were worn in reunions, assemblies, and ceremonies.

The boots of the present day are high and low. Boots are better than shoes, because they afford more protection for the feet, and strengthen the ankles and aid the step.

Independent of their incontestable utility, for a long time they were more governed by fashion than comfort. Instead of maintaining the foot, and protecting it against humidity and cold, they were only made to make the foot appear as small as possible. In general, shoes should be well adapted to the form of the feet and legs. As to the material used, it necessarily varies according to the climate

and season, as well as to the susceptibility
of individuals. One thing should be borne
in mind, that they are made to protect the
feet and preserve the health.

I have already spoken of the disadvantages
resulting from high-heeled boots. Having
passed in review what touches the physical
education, perhaps it is permissible to con-
clude with a few words on the education
properly called by Montaigne *the moral insti-
tution of man.*

An educated man is not always a learned
man : the perfection of education is instruction mingled with politeness, culture of mind
joined to culture of character. Use, example,
and acts are the best masters in education.

Education begins from the cradle. Woman
is man's first teacher. The happiest education is that which retains traces of the gentle
and affectionate authority of woman. A
child grows up under the gentle, benevolent
authority of its mother. Ardent passions
are moderated, bad inclinations are corrected,
gentle qualities of heart and character are developed. Later on, when replaced by strange

authority, when the ideas are fully awakened, this early pious influence will continue to follow him on through life.

It is in early age that good examples and impressions seize the character and root themselves in the mind for a lifetime. Common education, it is said, is the prelude of life. A child destined to live the life of the world, should live in the world, and the world of youth is the college.

But is man destined to live in youth's world? Assuredly not. The world of youth is the world of frank simplicity, natural ideas, and generous instincts.

In the world of youth characters find all their purity, as well as all their roughness. College education is indispensable to youth. There the ideas enlarge, the sentiment of justice becomes developed, the passions are controlled, and often, by force of discipline, deadened; generosity and love of country are also there developed. To moderate that exuberance in point of view of men's society, that individual action, so salutary, requires another thing. Is common education really a necessary preparation, particularly efficacious, to acts and moral duties of social life? I do not believe it. If it is, there one finds the means of crushing vanity and pride, stimulating laziness, moderating jealousy and anger. It is not there that the child will find the germ of that gentle, benevolent charm, if for no other reason than that he has not reached maturity ; later, he will learn the part he has to take in life.

Such are the mutual wants of society. Then college education should be moderated by family education ; in all times and everywhere it should be present with its influence. Later, with reason and heart the child becomes a man, and will freely take his place in social life, and occupy it with as much dignity as if he had submitted longer to the tender maternal authority of family education.

I have had occasion to mention several times, in this little book, the influence, examples, and acts of private life, and the indelible impression they leave on the mind of youth. The movements and attitudes of the body awaken correlative sentiments ; and if from our attitudes spring our instincts, said Gratiolet, one will soon understand the importance that respectable people attach to good manners. Good manners are forms of virtue, and he who in infancy has contracted the habit of good language, will not easily speak the language of evil.

Malebranche tells of a young servant who assisted a surgeon to bleed the feet of his master; the moment the lance touched the skin, he was seized with a pain so acute in his own foot, that had the operation been performed on him, he could not have felt it more than he did.

The sight of joy inspires the idea of joy, that of grief oppresses the heart, that of anger alters the traits, etc.

In all forms, with few exceptions, when later regrettable imperfections are to be deplored, parents are most to blame for neglecting their duty during infancy and youth.

CHAPTER VIII.

PERFUMES AND ODORS.

AMONG mankind, the sense of smell is less perfect than among most animals, for with them it is sometimes their principal instinctive organ. Odor is for man a source of pleasure. Rousseau and Zimmerman said that odor is the sense of imagination. Perfumes add to the advantage of beauty. The care which certain women take to perfume themselves, is a proof that voluptuous ideas are united to flowers, perfumes, etc. "*Fulcite me floribus, stipate me malis quia amore langueo,*" cried the young Shunamite to his companions in the "Canticle of Canticles" ("surround me with flowers, for I die of love)." The poets attributed to odor the power of inspiring in the soul a gentle intoxication.

However, to some persons, all odors are disagreeable, and the fragrance of flowers has often had dangerous effects. Above all things, one should avoid sleeping in a room where there are flowers.

The Marshal de Richelieu, during his declining years, lived in a most fragrant atmosphere, wafted by bellows through his apartment; and incredible to state, to this day there are habits that approach this extravagant luxury. I saw in Paris, a few years since, a lady who passed the greater part of her time on a sofa, in the midst of the most fragrant flowers, and who slept continually in an apartment filled with flowers and plants. After a short visit to this lady, I left with a headache, a sick stomach, and all symptoms of real poison; while she lived for years in that atmosphere—an existence which cannot be explained, unless her sense of smell was completely deadened, a thing observed among persons, who, by profession or habit, live amidst odors.   There are some very odd examples, a repulsion for such and such a perfume — or even for the mildest fragrance.

Many persons are disagreeably impressed by the smell of flaxseed. Orfila tells of a lady who became so overpowered with its smell, that she swooned, and had tumefaction of the face.   Many persons who dislike odors consider them dangerous.   It is all imagination.   Dr. Capellini tells of a lady who could not suffer the odor of a rose, and fell ill on receiving the visit of a lady friend who wore one; yet that fatal flower was artificial. Perfumes, 'tis true, have served to disguise and even compose poisons.

The ancients were refined in the art of mysterious killing.   In the midst of most absurd stories, which tradition tells us, many are proven true.   Agreeable odors are far from producing bad effects. "Odors," said Hippolyte Cloquet, "seem to change the nature of ideas, and vivify the thoughts."

Who has not more than once, like J. J. Rousseau, felt a universal moral and physical

9

satisfaction on breathing the air of the country filled with the fragrance of flowers? Who has not, when breathing the fresh air of spring, felt its gentle influence in the midst of the balmy atmosphere, and been pleased to remember, in a happy though melancholy contemplation, the image of a friend who is no more, or form for the future projects of happiness that ambition cannot poison with its lying tendency.

Perfumes have various origins. The temples of the ancients, the first churches, were always infected by emanations from the animals sacrificed, and bodies interred therein. They destroyed these disagreeable odors by burning incense and perfuming the altars. Moses carefully prescribed the perfume which should fill the tabernacle with its aromas; it was a mixture reserved to God. Another origin is more poetic—that they received life from the sunshine, and rose with it to perfume the air.

Purification, unctions of oil, perfumes, and ablutions formed the basis of ancient culture. The Chinese used perfumes for domestic use as well as pleasure. Whatever may be their origin, these perfumes were burned before the gods in all the temples.

Myrrh and incense were among the presents that the Wise Men offered the Messiah. Moses taught the Egyptian priests and scholars the science of perfumes. The Bible and its commentaries contain numerous cosmetic formulas which are in use at the present day. For a long time hygienic prescriptions were disguised under a religious form. The custom of using fragrant substances is established in our churches, but not so much carried on as formerly. At the baptism of Clovis fragrant tapers were burned ; and the Roman church about that time made so great a use of perfume, that she had lands in Syria and other Oriental provinces which were expressly used for the cultivation of perfumes. The wealthy Greeks had perfuming pans to send forth fragrance while they feasted. From Greece they spread to Rome. Notwithstanding their sale was rigorously prohibited, their use continued to increase. They employed them in the most extravagant manner in their baths, sleeping-rooms, and beds ; they also wasted them in all public feasts. The air was embalmed with their vapors when Pompey entered Naples and Antony Alexandria. Plutarch tells us of a supper given by Otho to Nero. On all sides tubes of gold and silver, filled with perfumes of great price, sent forth such a profuse odor as to moisten the repast. At the funeral of his wife Poppæa, Nero had burned on the funeral pile more incense than Arabia could produce in a year. France in its turn increased and opposed without ever doing away with it, even when in the midst of a thousand vicissitudes.

Nevertheless, since the time of Marie Antoinette it has sustained a real importance in ceremonies and feasts, as well as in particular uses. Napoleon I. was very fond of perfumes ; he sprinkled himself with eau de cologne every morning. The Empress Josephine was passionately fond of flowers.

We are not, however, like the ancients, connoisseurs of pleasure, nor, like them, do

we passionately seek perfumes.   But we do
generally admit this maxim, that *sensation is
as necessary to the soul as exercise is to the
body.*

CHAPTER IX.

COSMETICS—Resumed.

COSMETICS comprise all substances designed to preserve and restore if not aid beauty. I have already given several formulas, with their special application. But cosmetics are so numerous, that it rests with one to choose among those that hygiene recommends, by indicating the object for which they are intended.

COSMETICS FOR THE SKIN.

COLD CREAM.

Almond Oil........................	5 ounces.
Spermaceti...................	1 ounce, 1 drachm.
White Wax........................	½ ounce.
Rose-water	1 ounce.
Eau de Cologne....................	2 drachms.
Tincture of Benzoin...............	18 grains.

COLD CREAM A LA ROSE.

Almond Oil......................	1 pint.
Rose-water......................	1 pint.
White Wax......................	7 drachms.
Spermaceti......................	7 drachms.
Essence of Rose..................	16 grains.

CUCUMBER POMADE.

Essence of Cucumber......	
Spermaceti...............	Almost equal quantities.
Fresh Lard..............	

COLD CREAM À LA VIOLETTE.

Oil of Violets..................	1 pint.
Violet Water..................	1 pint.
Wax..........................	7 drachms.
Spermaceti....................	7 drachms.
Essence of Almonds.............	5 drops.

Mix carefully.

SULTAN'S CREAM.

Oil of Benzoin	1 ounce.
Oil of Poppies..................	2 drachms.
White Wax......................	1 drachm.
Spermaceti......................	1 drachm.
Flowers of Benzoin..............	1 drachm.
Extract of Orange Flowers..1 scruple,	7 grains.
Blancs de Perles................	1 ounce.
Essence of Roses................	9 grains.

Almonds, pounded	2 ounces.
Venetian Lact	¼ ounce.
Peruvian Balm	2 grains.

Mix according to art.

MILK OF ROSES.

Sweet Almonds, pounded		2 ounces.
Rose-water		3 gills.
Alcohol	1 ounce,	2 drachms.
Windsor Soap		1 drachm.
White Wax		1 drachm.
Sweet Oil		1 drachm.
Essence of Bergamot		1 drachm.
Essence of Lavender		9 grains.
Essence of Roses		5 grains.

Mix it in pure water, and anoint or bathe the face and neck.

GLYCERINE LOTION.

Orange-flower Water	1 quart.
Glycerine	¼ pound.
Borax	7 drachms.

COSMETIC LOTION.

Black Cherry Water, distilled	1 quart.
Cucumber Pomade	3 ounces.
Almond Soap	4 drachms.

Mix the soap with the pomade, and add water by degrees.

GOWLAND LOTION.

Bitter Almonds	3 ounces.
Water	1 pint.
Corrosive Sublimate	2 grains.
Salts of Ammonia	1 scruple.
Alcohol	4 drachms.
Black Cherry Water	4 drachms.

MILK OF ALMOND LOTION.

Pounded Almonds	4 ounces.
Rose-water	½ pint.
Corrosive Sublimate	3 grains.
Carbonate of Potash	11 grains.

Mix well.

COSMETIC WATER.

Bitter Almonds	1 pound.
Water	2 quarts.

Distil, and add—

Vinegar Rosat	1 quart.
Essence of Raspberry	1 drachm.
Essence of Honey	1 ounce.
Essence of Jessamine	1 ounce, 4 drachms.

LAVENDER WATER.

Oil of Lavender	4 ounces.
Alcohol, rectified	2 quarts.
Rose-water	½ pint.

9*

The following is excellent:

EAU DE COLOGNE.

Alcohol	8 pints.
Volatile Oil of Lemon.................	1 ounce.
Volatile Oil of Cedrat................	8 drachms.
Volatile Oil of Lavender.............	1 drachm.
Volatile Oil of Bergamot.............	6 drachms.
Tincture of Benzoin.........	1 ounce, 3 drachms.

Strain it, and let it stand for some time.

AROMATIC VINEGAR FOR THE TOILETTE.

Camphorated Vinegar...............	2½ pints.
Camphor	1 ounce.

Mix well.

CUCUMBER VINEGAR.

Cucumbers...........................	2 ounces.
Strong Vinegar	1 quart.

Let it steep twenty-five days; then strain it.

RASPBERRY VINEGAR.

Vinegar (strong)...................	1 quart.
Raspberries, either fresh or dry.......	3 pints.

Let it steep fifteen days, then strain.

ROSE VINEGAR.

Vinegar (strong)...................	6 gills.
Red Roses..........................	1 ounce.

Steep eight days, and strain.

VIRGINAL VINEGAR.

White Vinegar.....................⎫ Equal parts.
Benzoin, pulverized................⎭

   Steep it eight days, and strain; drop it in the water
for the toilette, and it becomes milky white.
These vinegars are excellent for clearing the skin,
and making it firm and solid.

POWDER FOR PARTS THAT ARE CHAFED.

Powdered Lycopode.................... 1 ounce.
Oxide of Zinc........................ ½ ounce.
   Mix them. With the aid of a puff or hare's foot,
touch the parts chafed by walking.

BLANC DE PERLES (FOR THE THEATRE).

Rose or Orange-flower Water............ 1 pint.
Oxide of Bismuth.........:.... 3 ounces, 4 drachms.
   Pound them very fine, and mix.

ROUGES DE TOILETTE.

Rouges de Toilette are made of various colors by mixing
different proportions of pure carmines with pulverized talc.
1 to 2 scruples of carmine for 2 to 3 ounces of talc.

COSMETICS FOR THE HAIR.

Pure Marrow............................	4 ounces.
Oil of Almonds........................	4 ounces.
Oil of Palm............................	2 drachms.
Essence of Cloves.....................	4 grains.
Essence of Bergamot..................	1 drachm.
Essence of Lemon......................	2 drachms.

POMADE OF BEAR'S OIL.

Oil à la Rose.........................	1 drachm.
Orange Flower........................	1 drachm.
Sweet Oil.............................	1 drachm.
Oil of Tuberoses......................	1 drachm.
Oil of Jessamine......................	1 drachm.
Oil of Almonds............. 1 ounce,	1 drachm.
Essence of Bergamot..................	1 scruple.
Essence of Cloves....................	18 grains.
Fresh Lard...........................	2 ounces.

Steep all the pomades together, then mix the oil and add the essences.

POMADE TO PREVENT BALDNESS.

Extract of Quinine...................	1 scruple.
Sweet Almond Oil.....................	2 drachms.
Beef Marrow..........................	6 drachms.
Essence of Bergamot..................	6 drops.
Peruvian Balm........................	8 drops.

Mix with care, and anoint the head on retiring.

The following oils are excellent to prevent falling of the hair :

> Beef Marrow,
> Oil of Almonds,
> Oil of Nuts.
> Mix, and use at will.

MACASSAR OIL.

Oil of Turnsole	3 ounces.
Goose Oil	4 drachms.
Storax Liquid	
Essence of Thyme	} 2 drachms each.
Balm of Cocoa	
Essence of Neroli	} 1 drachm each.
Essence of Roses	
Peruvian Balm	11 grains.

Let all the ingredients steep and remain in a moderately warm place.

PERFUME FOR REMOVING GREASE FROM THE HAIR.

Wheat Bran, perfectly dry	1 pound.
Iris Powder	2 ounces.
Pass through a sieve.	

Powder the hair at night, brush next morning, and use a fine comb. This perfume is often put in little scent bags and worn under the armpits. To preserve certain conditions of the hair, retain its lustre, and keep it in curl, there are various cosmetics called *fixateurs* or bandolines.

Adraganth Gum......................	2 drachms.
Water	1 pint.

Let it steep five or six hours; strain it through a piece of muslin, and add—

Alcohol.............................	3 ounces.
Rose-water	10 drops.

One may also use psyllrum gum; and better still, quince seed with a little eau de cologne.

POMADE TO PREVENT ALOPECY.

Precipitate of Sulphur in a hydrate state,	1 drachm.
Prepared Beef Marrow................	4 drachms.
Rum................................	2 drachms.

Mix, and aromatize with Balm of Tolu.

SCHNEIDER'S POMADE.

Lemon Juice.......................	1 drachm.
Extract of Quinine.................	2 drachms.
Tincture of Cantharides............	1 drachm.
Oil of Cedrate....................	1 scruple.
Oil of Bergamot....................	1 grain.
Beef Marrow.......................	3 ounces.

Mix well, and after having washed the scalp well with pure soap and water, anoint it with this pomade.

STEIGE'S POMADE.

Balm of Cocoa..............	1 ounce, 2 drachms.
Quinine,...........................	1 drachm.
Olive Oil.........................	5 drachms.
Tannin	2 grains.
Aromatic Alcohol...................	2 drachms.

Mix well; anoint the head morning and night.

POMADE TO BLACKEN THE HAIR.

Acetate of Silver...................	2 drachms.
Cream of Tartar...................	2 drachms.
Ammonia.........................	4 drachms.
Lard.............................	4 drachms.

Apply this pomade with the aid of a brush. To remove the stains it may leave on the fingers or forehead, use a little solution of iodide of potassium or hyposulphate of soda or chloride.

WATER FOR DYEING THE HAIR BLACK.

HAIR DYE.

Oil of Wax.......................	8 ounces.
Gall Nuts........................	½ ounce.

Boil till the nuts break, and add:

Basalt...........................	1 drachm.
Gem Salt........................	1 drachm.
White Wax.......................	1 drachm.
Cloves...........................	1 scruple.
Pulverized Alum...................	1 drachm.

Boil it a second time for five minutes, then strain.

BLONDE HAIR DYE.

White Wine.......................... 3 gills.
Rhubarb (dry)...................... 5 ounces.

Boil them together until reduced to half the quantity. Strain it, and wash the hair, and let it dry.

ANOTHER.

Distilled Water of Plantain........... 1 gill.
Nitrate of Silver.................... 2 drachms.
Bismuth............................ 4 drachms.
Acetate of Iron..................... 2 drachms.

Mix. Bathe the hair, after having removed all grease.

MINERAL DYE.

Acetate of Silver.................... 7 drachms.
Rose-water.......................... 1 gill.

Before using this water, the head should be washed in a solution of alkaline of soda or potassium. When the hair is well dried, apply the dye with an old soft tooth-brush. This dye will take effect in a few hours.

COSMETICS FOR THE MOUTH.

TOOTH POWDER.

Calcinated Magnesia.................. ½ ounce.
Sulphate of Quinine.................. 9 grains.
Carmine.................... Sufficient quantity.
Essence of Mint..................... 3 drops.

TORIAC'S POWDER.

Carbonate of Lime.................. 1 drachm.
Magnesia.......................... 2 drachms.
Sugar............................. 1 drachm.
Pulverized Cream of Tartar.......... 1 scruple.
Essence of Mint..................... 1 drop.

ENGLISH TOOTH POWDER.

White Chalk........................ ½ pound.
Pulverized Camphor................. 3 ounces.
    Cork tight in small bottles.

CORAL TOOTH POWDER.

Pulverized Coral.................... 1 ounce.
Lake Carmine....................... 1 grain.
Sulphate of Quinine................. 1 grain.
Volatile Oil of Mint................. 2 drops.
    Mix well together, and make a fine paste.

ELIXIR FOR THE TEETH.

Distilled Alcohol of Rosemary......... ½ pint.
Camomile Root (bruised)............. 1 ounce.

Steep and strain. Mix this elixir with double the quantity of water to rinse the mouth.

A complete list of washes, elixirs, powders, opiates, and dentrifices, would be interminable. Therefore I give a list of those mostly employed.

COSMETICS FOR A BAD BREATH.

Brandy............................. 1 gill.
Mint-water, or Spearmint Tea........ 1 gill.
Chloride of Soda.................... 6 drachms.
    Mix.

LOZENGES FOR THE BREATH.

Powdered Coffee............ 1 ounce, 3 drachms.
Vegetable Charcoal............... .. ½ ounce.
Powdered Sugar..................... ½ ounce.
Vanilla............................ ½ ounce.
Gum Arabic............... Sufficient quantity.
    Make them each of about eighteen grains, take five or six a day, and the breath will become sweet.

COSMETICS FOR THE HANDS.

POWDER FOR THE HANDS.

Powdered Horse-chestnuts...........	⅞ pound.
Carbonate of Potassium.............	2 drachms.
Bitter Almond Powder..............	½ pound.
Iris...............................	1 ounce.
Essence of Bergamot................	1 drachm.

Mix.

ALMOND PASTE FOR THE HANDS.

Almonds, sweet, peeled.............	¼ pound.
Almonds, bitter....................	¼ pound.
Lemon-juice.......................	2 ounces.
Milk..............................	1 ounce.
Sweet Oil of Almonds..............	3 ounces.
Brandy............................	1 gill.

Mix with great care.

POWDER FOR THE NAILS.

The best is composed of pure oxide of tin, perfumed with essence of lavender, and colored with carmine.

It is applied on the nails with the finger, or a little brush covered with leather—called in French *polissoir.*

CHAPTER X.

VARIOUS PERFUMES.

ESSENCES FOR THE HANDKERCHIEF.

ROYAL ESSENCE.

Ambergris	2 scruples.
Musk	1 scruple.
Civet	1 grain.
Volatile Oil of Roses	1 grain.
Volatile Oil of Cinnamon	1 grain.
Oil of Rhodes' Wood	1 grain.
Oil of Orange Flowers	1 grain.
Carbonate of Potash	1 grain.
Alcohol	3 ounces.

Let it steep fifteen days, and strain it.

TRIPLE EXTRACT OF ROSE.

Alcohol, rectified	1 gill.
Essence of Roses	3 ounces.

Mix. For the handkerchief.

EXTRACT OF AMBER.

Triple Extract of Rose...............	3 gills.
Tincture of Ambergris...............	6 gills.
Essence of Musk....................	3 drachms.
Extract of Vanilla..................	7 drachms.

Mix.

This perfume has such a powerful odor, that the handkerchief, once saturated with it, retains the perfume even after it is washed.

TINCTURE OF MUSK.

Musk in Grains......................	2 drachms.
Rectified Alcohol...................	5 gills.

Let it remain six months in a mild temperature, then strain it.   This extract is used to mix all others.

SCENT BAGS.

Cassia Flower-tops.	} Equal parts
Iris Powder.......................	

Mix.

SACHET À LA HELIOTROPE.

Iris Powder......	2 pounds.
Powdered Rose-leaves...............	1 pound.
Fev. de Tonka, in powder...........	6 ounces.
Vanilla Husks......................	3 ounces.
Musk, in Grains....................	2 drachms.
Essence of Almonds................	5 drops.

Mix it, and pass through a large sieve.

This is one of the best sachets.

COSMETICS FOR THE BATH.

Pure Vinegar, poured in the bath......... ¼ Pint.

It tones the skin, and aids the pores.

The following bath is called Modesty's Bath, because the women who were in the habit of using it, in Catholic countries, confessed in it, and received calls:

MODESTY'S BATH.

Sweet Almonds, hulled, pounded.......	8 ounces.
Œnula Campana......................	1 pound.
White Onions.......................	1 ounce.
Flaxseed...........................	1 pint.
Marsh-mallow Root..................	1 ounce.
Spur-nuts..........................	1 pound.

Pound them all well together, make a paste, put it in three little linen or cotton bags, throw it in the bath, and it will dissolve with a little compression.

This formula may be replaced by others more simple; for instance, by putting a sufficient quantity of almond paste to make the water turbid, and give it a milky appearance.

BRAN BATH.

Water......................	Sufficient quantity
Bran.............................	3 pounds.

Boil them.   Place in the bath.

EMOLLIENT BATH.

Emollient Spices.....................	4 pounds.
Flaxseed...........................	½ pound.
Water.............................	5 quarts.

Boil all together, and add it to the bath.

Aromatic baths are prepared with an infusion or decoction of aromatic plants.

Lavender leaves and flowers were very much employed in former times for perfuming the water of the bath ; from that it derives its generic name of "*lavandula.*"

Tincture of alcohol is also used as an ablution.

THE END.

THE ART OF PLEASING:

DEDICATED TO THE

PRETTY WOMEN OF ALL COUNTRIES.

BY

ERNEST FEYDEAU.

TRANSLATED FROM THE ORIGINAL FRENCH.

NEW YORK:

G. W. Carleton & Co., Publishers.

PARIS: LEVY FRERES.

M.DCCC.LXXIV.

Maclauchlan, Printer and Stereotyper,
56, 58 & 60 Park St., N. Y.

CONTENTS.

The Art of Pleasing.

CHAPTER I.

ONE of the sweetest dreams of my literary life was to found a fashion journal. I hasten to declare that I had not the slightest intention to imitate, in any way, the little illustrated papers, that are known to occupy themselves with such matter. My magazine, published in octavo form and appearing once a week, directed by myself alone, would have no plates nor advertisements. According to my idea, it should be conceived and executed by the aid of God, less in a commercial point of view than in a didactic and literary form. I would

have endeavored to make it extremely interesting, nay, even amusing—and that would
not have been difficult for me, because we
generally draw from what pleases us, and I
have ever possessed a decided inclination for
everything that pertains to the taste, care,
and adornment of the fair sex. The only
thing that prevented me from realizing this
charming dream was the absolute want of
capital. Unfortunately, one cannot found a
review without money. The printer, the
paper dealer, and capitalist, have rarely the
patience to wait for subscriptions. It was
not sufficient, then, to have an excellent literary idea. A moneyed man must be found.
The capital I required was not an immense
sum—fifty thousand francs—but it was as
difficult for me to furnish that amount as
though it were fifty millions. To all my de-
mands, the infamous capitalists that I count
among the number of my friends, and that
the Commune neglected to shoot—it did not
do great good, that Commune!—invariably
gave the same dilatory reply: "My idea was
excellent, and would have the most legiti-

mate success ; that there was no one worthy the name of woman who would refuse to become a subscriber and constant reader. But the war—business continuation of the Provisory—in short, want of funds.'' And I !— there I was, Simple Simon as before.

Again : the motive that prompted me to propose to my friends that which was so contrary to my tastes and habits, did not arise from the desire to make concurrence to any of the different papers of the same nature then in existence. I find them simply loathsome without exception. The best managed among them is not fit to read. Not one among them has a line that can in any way interest the most beautiful, the most interesting part, of the human race. By way of retaliation, one would think they all were united to treat in the most vulgar language, subjects that could only captivate the scum of dress-makers. They contain nothing for intelligent women. It does not interest women in high life how many flounces or ruches such a dress-maker uses on her customers' dresses. That question, and all others of the same type,

merits a place only among the advertisements
of Houses to let, and Horses to sell, etc. It is
then a matter to create a journal, ameliorate
the education, and form and develop the female taste, to teach them to care and adorn
their precious person, and bring to light
all their advantages. It is a question then to
prevent young, pretty women the world over
from going to extremes in toilettes, that unfortunately has during the past ten years
done them no small wrong in the minds of
men. It is regretable, but not useless to-day
to state—It is time to lecture women on the
art of not making themselves ugly. I am
aware they do it in the praiseworthy view of
pleasing us, and that touches me to tears.
But I prefer to see them have a little more
self-respect. And that is why I had, and
still have, the idea to incite and aid them
to it.

Here let not ill-balanced minds object that
a man of letters, serious as I am known to be,
has no quality to advise on such delicate,
tender matter as the fancies of taste, *bon ton*,
and adjustment of female hygiene and ap-

parel. Women are jealous, and seek constantly to injure one another. I believe that
all of them, even the most illustrious, are
absolutely incapable of taking hold of the
entire question of dress or fashion, or to use
the least philosophy in regard to toilette or
preservation of beauty. Without daring to
criticise them, I affirm that they have a way
of judging and admiring and liking themselves that is not good. I do not find them
competent for anything that shows their sex
to advantage.

That belongs to the men. In short, to return to what concerns me, it is because I am
a man I love women. And to love them is
to advise them ; and because I am serious, I
can treat all matters seriously, even matters
that may appear ridiculous in the eyes of
superficial people. It is because I am grave
that people will listen to me when I speak of
dress. It is not necessary to be up in letters,
nor be a French dress-maker, in order to
speak of the thousand pretty things that
ever interest women. I pretend to interest
them by speaking to them intelligently, in
10*

good taste, of things that please them.   I can
do so completely, because my inclinations all
tend there ; and let it not be forgotten that the
renovations that have recently taken place in
the costume of women, were not begun by
women, but by men, whose names deserve to
be attached to that renovation: three men
—three artists in this sense—namely, Worth,
Aurelly, Pingat.   The first particularly, in
opening to Paris special studios consecrated to
female dress, has done more in a few years to
direct fashion, taste, and comfort combined,
than the most renowned female artists could
do in a century.   Worth is celebrated the
world over, and he merits to be.   Nothing
is wanting to his reputation.   He has been
cut up, ridiculed, and envied—as many other
inventors and men of genius have wished
to be.   Of an inventive mind, and, above all,
careful of grace and beauty, he has not allowed that goddess, Fashion, ever inconstant,
sometimes ridiculous, to become absurd, as
she often is, in the sense of ugliness and
deformity.   With a form before him, and a
few yards of stuff chosen with discretion,

and a paper of pins, he invents, composes, and draws from his inspiration.

I must stop, because in the terrible epoch in which we have the misfortune to live, it has become radically impossible to speak the praises of any one, even of a dress-maker, without being immediately suspected, by pure men, to be guilty of the crime of writing an interested advertisement. I do not think, however, that Worth is any more in need of an advertisement than I am ; I will cease speaking of him. The little I have said was said to prove that it is indispens-able to be a man, in order to dress a woman well. But before pushing this demonstra-tion, I must retrace my steps, so as to better show how great would have been the oppor-tunity in the paper I had the idea of starting. Let my fair readers be assured that I had not the slightest idea of copying Sardou, and, like him, celebrate "*La Sainte Mousseline.*" I am above all things a serious man, fond of luxury, art, and beauty.

I have a horror of the vulgar. I do not like the simple, nor the economical. I hate

muslin, Indian stuffs, and all those common
things that please our friends the Prussians.
And it is precisely because I am so, that
I boast, and that I need no small amount
of philosophy to swallow the fashions and
evolutions that the fickle goddess has been
delivered up to during the past twenty
years; that the desire to learn has pushed
me to occupy myself with the subject.
Women submitted then to the despotism
known by the name of crinoline. They suspended from their waists those horrid iron
cages, sometimes covered with cloth, making
them look like furies.

In spite of all the respectful remarks
that sensible men permitted themselves to
address them, they invariably replied, with
the air of victims, that there was no possible
way of being decently dressed without crinoline; that the iron cage alone could give
them grace and charm, and that men must
make the best of it.

CHAPTER II.

T was in vain that we objected with all
sorts of circumlocution ; even praying
was of no avail.

Eve, our great-great-grandmother, was
content to be dressed with her flowing blonde
hair and a fig-leaf. The women of by-gone
days, in all countries and at all times—even in
France—dispensed with crinoline, and were
none the less charming. But that does not
influence women of the present day, nor con-
vince them of the ugliness of the above-
named cages ; and in spite of their practical
good sense, they carry it to excess, their
dress resembling a sun umbrella, and making
them look like flutes.

I, humble philosopher as I am, admire all
this. I admire many other changes too,
politically. Even now, a certain timidity
prevails that one hides one's hair. The devil
may know—I do not ! They twist their chignons on the top of their heads. At the sea-

side, and in the country, they wear them full length, triumphantly attached behind the head; in the city, the supreme elegance consists in giving them the superb color of the yolk of an egg. So all ladies' heads have at once assumed that color; yet there are a few of our lady friends who prefer "cow's-tail color:" but they are few, much to their credit.

I have not finished. The most beautiful part of the human race, to speak in the classics, have, thanks to man, abstained from dyeing their hair. But once started on a certain course, it is hard to leave off. At the present day, women paint their eyes, eyelashes, lips, and even their cheeks, with a powder resembling flour. There are many to be seen daily on the promenade, who use a little carmine on their ears and on the edges of their nostrils. Their faces are disgusting, that a respectable man, when he sees them, can feel no other desire than that of washing it.

CHAPTER III.

ET us pass on. Some fools believed till now, that Nature had given us feet to walk. It was an error. Women have proven that. We have feet to slide with, nothing else. And the proof is, that not content to wear pointed heels two inches high, which seemed reasonable, the beautiful partners of our joys and sorrows conceived the idea of placing the heels—not where Nature intended, at the *calcaneum*, but just in the middle of the sole of the foot.

To this I willingly agree—there is nothing in the world so ugly—I will use the word so ignoble—as a pair of large flat feet ; above all, when they belong to a fat person, shod in prunella, it is horrible—enough to make the dogs in the street growl. Cannot one avoid one excess, without falling into another still worse? Between the heels placed on the soles of the feet, and cotton, satin, cloth, and

prunella, quite flat, I would choose absolutely
in favor of the former.

CHAPTER IV.

WILL stop, not wishing to have the
air of criticising a sex of which (praise
be to the shadow of Diogenes) it
would be very difficult for us to exist without.

Not having succeeded in founding a paper
whose whole view was nothing more than to
give a few good hints on the hygiene of taste
and toilette, without the least intention of at-
tacking its merits (they are always perfect),
or its character (it is alone worthy of praise),
nor to reform fancies, I will attempt in this
little volume, and in the most attractive form,
that which I would have done in my fashion
journal, if my lucky star and the state of fortune of my capitalists and friends had permitted me to start it.   Let no one hasten to

accuse me of frivolity, for nothing is frivolous in my opinion in what concerns women ; and after the events through which we have just passed, I esteem it a good thing to turn aside from politics, and talk of dress, so as not to lose our habits on the subject, since the Prussians are no longer here to listen to us.

La Bruyère, who was certainly a writer of genius, though wanting in a little gallantry, said,* " I will be imprudent enough to judge the sex, but I will study them after this precept.   Of all the members that Nature has given us, there are none so delicate, more elegant, more supple, more ingeniously disposed, than the feet.   Whosoever has taken pains to study the contexture, truly marvellous, of these members, in which the bones and muscles are harmoniously united to support the weight of the body and furnish the means of moving with elasticity and ease, cannot fail to feel an ardent admiration for the wisdom of the Creator in everything.   Ah well !   It is sad to state, but in France to-day, on account of

* *La Bruyère's " Character of . Women."*

the profound imbecility of chiropodists and the perfect stupidity of shoemakers, one of the rarest, most difficult things to meet, is a pair of pretty feet on a lady.

Here it is necessary to explain the exact sense of the word beauty. A vulgar prejudice has been laid on that observation though full of justice, that states : "The constitution of a woman is more delicate than that of a man ; the fibres of the female form are more frail and of a weaker tissue than in man ; a vulgar prejudice, did I say, absolutely declares that female perfection consists in smallness of stature, and of the parts of the body. There is nothing more absurd. One has only to consult the engravings in fashion journals, to have an idea of the elegant monstrosities invented by this prejudice : the tiny hands, imperceptible feet, eyes larger than the mouth, a slim little waist in strange contrast with the exaggerated hips and broad shoulders—these are the horrible beauties which the generality of women envy, and the public laud. Artists, who are the only persons competent in this question, de-

clare that beauty consists in the harmony of
all parts of a subject, as well as in the perfect equilibrium of its proportions. And there
is nothing more true than this assertion.
Hence it is quite indispensable that the eyes
of a woman should be smaller than her mouth ;
that her waist should be neither thick nor
thin, and yet retain flexibility and grace,
which are the principal attractions ; they
should be in just proportion with the other
parts of her body ; the hands and feet should
harmonize regularly with the arms and legs.
In brief : a large woman, to be perfectly
made, should have large hands and feet. If
she has not, so much the worse for her : she
is not perfect.

The beauty of each organ does not consist in its dimensions, but in its special form.
A large woman who has little feet, particularly if they are well made, is certainly less
displeasing and more agreeable to see than
one with the feet of an orang-outang. Yet
that does not make her perfect. I repeat,
beauty of form is this : A high instep, a
round, plump foot, with ivory skin, the toes

slightly separated, the first toe being larger and rounder than the others; the blue veins showing, and the toe-nails bright and polished, with a rosy tint. Then the foot is handsome; if in proportion with the rest of the body, it is simply perfect. All that is needed is to measure it.

CHAPTER V.

THE ancient Egyptians, Greeks, Romans—all of whom think there is nothing debasing in paying particular attention to the least details of private life, favored as they were by the mildness of their climate—attached great value to the beauty of their wives and daughters.

In their estimation, female feet, by their contexture, delicacy, and use, were in greater danger of being spoiled than any other parts of the body, and hence should be particularly cared for. Women walked little.

The wives of Mussulmen live retired in their homes, where amusements and pleasures are rarely wanting ; have their fine soft carpets, on which they repose their naked feet.

The study of antiquity shows us that the shoes of women in different countries, all over the world, were made to present the beauty of the feet. The Egyptian women wore a kind of sandal of wood, with a little band of skin across the instep, the point of the sandal turned up, to preserve the toes.

The women of Assyria wore silk sandals, adorned with pearls : the Greek and Roman ladies wore exquisite sandals, whose great merit consisted in not showing any part of the foot.

The same are those which are seen on the feet of Diana, one of the most beautiful statues in the Museum of the Louvre : "Diana and the Deer." I must not omit to mention a fact that proves that the Roman women, if Ovid is to be believed, like the Parisian ladies of our days, were inclined to ruin their feet with the view of making them small. The poet pretends that some of them wore shoes of white skin, that so pressed their feet as to enter in the flesh.*

That is more than binding them in purple, of which Virgil tells in his Elegies.

But I cannot here discuss the history of shoes, worn by all the people on the face of the globe. The only thing that I am interested in to repeat now, is the intelligent care that the women of antiquity took of their feet.

The greatest part of the infirmities and deformities that injure the feet of women, come, as I have stated, from the desire to make them small if they are not small. Let it be understood, however, when I say feet should be small, that they should always be in proportion with the rest of the body; when I say a woman, to be handsome, should have large feet, I mean reasonably so. I do not mean a plantation of flesh without bone or muscle, with knotty toes that look more fit for Prussian dairy-maids. I simply wish to say that the harmony of proportion is the most imperious condition of beauty.

* *Ovid's " Art of Love,"* iii. v. 271.

CHAPTER VI.

UT to return to women afflicted with the mania of wearing tight shoes. They not only spoil the feet, but they injure and irritate them, and do injury to the general health and complexion of the woman who wears them, giving her the air of a person suffering from a colic, and will erelong render a woman peevish, cross, and continually out of humor. It is tight shoes that make the feet ugly ; bring on bunions, corns, and other deformities and enlargements of the joints. Every woman who insists on wearing tight shoes is preparing herself for a most miserable existence ; I really believe it would be preferable for her to be blind, deaf, or stupid, rather than thus to poison her life.

An intelligent woman, careful of her beauty, and who respects herself, should have recourse to the chiropodist in an extreme necessity ; she should take care of her feet herself, by washing, brushing, filing, trimming or cutting them, and always keep the nails short and rounded, and keep them as neat as her hands. If she does not do it for the sake of the one she loves, she should do it for the sake of the art itself.

It is more shameful for a pretty woman to have a corn or bunion on her foot, than to deceive, without a good motive, her dearest lover.

And now I will discuss boots and shoes.

CHAPTER VII.

OMEN'S shoes should be always soft and easy ; not too easy. They should mould the feet in every sense of form. If I were not afraid of circulating a truth such as rendered so popular M. de la Palisse, I would say the best means for a woman to have good-fitting shoes, or better still, pretty feet (the latter being equally important), is to propose to her shoemaker the following conditions: First, take no notice of the ridiculous observations he makes, and do not fail to oppose him.

Women's shoemakers, like others, are all, or nearly all, a very ignorant class, without ideas, knowledge, or taste, the most of them Germans; and it is a rare thing to find them in keeping with their gallant trade. Shoemaker for pretty women! Is there in the world a more delightful trade for a sentimental soul! Unfortunately, with few exceptions, shoemakers are nothing less than unworthy intriguers. They think as little of deforming the feet of their charming customers, as I would of displeasing the King of Prussia. Therefore one should pay no attention to them, but enforce their orders and have their own way. Allowing that a woman has well-shaped feet—that is to say in just proportion to her stature; a little slim, hollow, slightly long, delicate, with round toes, each quite separated from the other—she should never wear a shoe that would apparently enlarge her foot. For this ·reason, boots made of

11

cloth, velvet, satin, or prunella should be pitilessly cast aside. Heavy kid boots for winter, and a lighter quality for summer, closely fitted to the foot, without bows of cloth, leather, rosettes, or any kind of trimming—this is the style of shoe a woman should wear. I need not add that these boots should have a heel about an inch high, not too pointed, nor placed too far back. With such a boot, a pretty young woman, provided she has a little wit and resolution, may face the greatest perils in life. Heaven aiding, she will always be sure to find something she can profit by in it.

CHAPTER VIII.

DURING the summer, low shoes of kid or goatskin, fine, supple, are very good for the city or country; they are elegant and convenient. Dress slippers should be made smaller in satin, silk, or fine cloth,

embroidered and trimmed with lace, and invariably the same color as the dress. An important condition I shall not. cease to repeat,
is, that while they fit snugly a pretty foot,
they should never be so tight as to impede
the step. Here an occasion presents itself to
say a few words on those slippers quite open
on the back. They are exceedingly convenient, and can never be too elegantly made.
Jordan, Dupuis, and Jacobs, all first-class
ladies' shoemakers, make very pretty ones,
of all colors and pretty materials—silk, embroidered in jet, trimmed with lace, etc.
There is no harm for a lady, anxious to
please, to wear them a little large. A pretty
young woman, taking her afternoon nap on
a warm summer's day, may at her pleasure
kick them off one after the other, with a
slight jerk. She can afterwards slip her feet
into them quite easily. I heard a story of a
beautiful young creole, who from sheer laziness or contempt for humanity made her
husband, a serious man, perform the pleasing task of putting on her slippers.

This must not be considered vain or silly

theory, because there is a charm about it
after all. It may prove profitable to the fair
sex, especially to some of my gentle readers,
who may deign to meditate a little on it.
How many young women I have known that
owed their success and fortune to a pretty
foot, well formed and correctly shod !

CHAPTER IX.

THE art of pleasing is not acquired by
experience or study. To possess this
precious art, which is the ambition of
all women, it is indispensable that Nature
should have accorded, in putting her in the
world, some choice happy tendencies to it.

An ugly, ill-formed woman may in vain
torture her imagination and spend her
money: it is not the hair-dresser, nor the
dress-maker, nor the enamelists themselves,
that can make a pretty woman of her. The
resources that we possess for remedying a

few of our physical defects and infirmities, are extremely limited.

We can teach them without fear of being taken for paradoxical. The surest means for a woman to acquire and preserve the gift of pleasing, is to be, if she can, always young, always pretty, always gentle, and always in good humor; thus she will ever be charming.

For several years, speaking in the classics, the sceptre of beauty, that until now belonged exclusively to the Parisian ladies, . seems to have passed into the hands of the American dames. It is not that the latter have more taste, more character, or more means than the former. It comes simply from the fact that the Anglo-Saxon race, being formed of the fusion of ten different races, renders it at present richer and higher endowed, under the triple force of health and beauty, than ours.

I will not speak of intellectual qualities, yet I have a right to speak of the taste, the tact, and the practical good sense of the *belles Yankees*—those fascinating women in whose veins able mycrographers might find some

English, German, French, Dutch, Spanish,
and Italian blood, and by close searching a
little particle of Indian and perhaps a drop
of Negro blood. Hence the Americans have
become handsomer, and gradually better
formed, than the French. This is a provoking fact for us without doubt, but it is now
affirmed henceforth, to express myself again
in the classics, that "the palm of Parisian
beauty belongs to them."

If on the Grand Avenue of the Champs
Elysées, at the hour of five P. M., you meet a
lady handsomely formed, elegantly and correctly dressed, large or small, generally tall,
with jet black hair or golden blonde, pretty
feet with good fitting shoes, a distinguished
air, graceful figure, beautiful eyes, fine teeth
—in short, one of those women who would
turn one's head with a nameless fascination,
that cannot be analyzed—you may rest assured that she was born on the banks of the
Ohio or the Delaware. The same at a ball or
the opera : if you see every one crowding the
passage to see a lady with a marvellous pair
of shoulders chastely *décolleté*, whose intel-

ligent look would bespeak her musical, whose gentle, graceful carriage attracts all eyes, and subjugates all hearts, you are sure to be informed that she is a resident of New York or Washington. The daughters of William Penn are all or nearly all syrens, who would charm the wise Ulysses himself, if he were to return to life, and permit himself to gaze upon them.

These reflections remind me that the other day, as I was parting with a young lady from Boston, who was sojourning in Paris, and who honored me with her friendship, during the half hour that I had the pleasure of conversing with her, she found means to avoid speaking of things that she knew would not interest me. I had just finished correcting the first proof-sheets of this book, so it formed the principal subject of our conversation, and my charming listener, while praising and complimenting me on it—compliments I feel glad to merit—asked permission to make a slight criticism.

" You have omitted only one extremely im‧portant thing," said she, with charming irony, "in your interesting remarks on ladies' shoes. It is the stockings and garters; they have also their merit and usefulness. I would advise you by all means to repair this absurd forgetfulness."

CHAPTER X.

O obey the recommendation of my fair reader who deigned to interest herself in my babbling, I will complete in ten lines what was omitted in the preceding chapter on ladies' shoes.

Every one knows the amusing reply of a marchioness of the *ancien régime* to one of her friends, who expressed astonishment on seeing her order her jeweller to make a pair of garter buckles enriched with diamonds. The friend said:

"Why spend money on such objects; they are never seen?"

" Who knows," replied the marchioness, "but one might meet some insolent observer ?"

Would it not, then, in view of some insolent observer, which is often possible, be indispensable that a lady's garters should be so elegant that anybody could be permitted the honor of admiring them. There are many ladies, at least so I am told, whose garters are made to match the color of each dress. They are certainly queens of the toilette, and if they are not Americans, they deserve to be.

The most indispensable quality for garters, is not to be too tight. They should rigidly support the stocking without stretching too much; I need not add that they should be invariably worn above the knee, and never below.

A woman who is guilty of tying her garter below the knee, is unworthy to live.

I know only three kinds of stockings fit for a respectable lady to wear:

1st. Balbriggan thread open-work, to show the roseate tints of the flesh.

11*

2d. Silk, flesh-color or pale rose, that shows the undulations of the muscles; but their great fault is that they hide the feet.

3d. Sky-blue silk, red and green, which some women have the bad taste to wear, should be cast aside with black ones, or be worn by market women, waiting-maids of the King of Prussia's court, or left to the wives of the Communists. But unfortunately hose and shoes are not enough to dress a woman. Her head-dress and clothing are indispensable articles of her costume.

Let us speak thereon.

CHAPTER XI.

NOTHING shows a pretty woman to better advantage than an elegant boot. A handsome dress has also many advantages. Still she is not complete with these.

Nothing crowns more graciously the facile structure of her carriage, than a tastefully made chapeau.

A grave question was raised in Paris a short time before the war, on the subject of ladies' dresses. It was discussed whether they should be worn long or short, slightly raised, or with flowing train. If they had deigned to consult me, unworthy as I am in so delicate and complex a question, I should have resolutely replied at the same time negatively and affirmatively.

In short, if there is nothing more elegant and graceful that shows the figure of a lady than a train of velvet or satin gliding over the carpet of a drawing-room, there is nothing more repugnant to see than the same train sweeping the dust and mud of the sidewalks —soiling the skirts and hose of the lady who wears it.

Street costumes should never be made on the same pattern as those intended for in-door wear. The most imperious rule to follow in the way of dress is this : the dress the best made, the easiest to wear, and the most agree-ble to see, will always be the one to mould exactly all parts of the female form.

A dress, to be well made, should have first a waist that perfectly moulds the form, shows the bust to advantage, and never wrinkles or creases on the back or shoulders. Even the movements of the legs in walking should show themselves through the skirt. A woman who walks all in one straight piece, like a board, without showing her movements or the plaits of her skirt, is simply a horrifying and ungraceful object.

CHAPTER XII.

LEAVE to the imagination of dressmakers, male and female, the care of varying the color, number, form, and adornment of all sorts of dresses. What matter to me? I am simply a philosopher. Without taking part, I indicate the principal traits that should guide the taste of each one

in the form of adjustment. I here lay down
the two fundamental principles in the question of dress :

·First, in-door dresses should never be
made on the same model as those for the
street.

Second, every dress, for whatever purpose
it is made, should, first of all, if it has the
honor of being worn by a well-formed
woman, exactly mould the form of her waist.

Rest certain that leg-of-mutton sleeves
were invented by a woman who had arms
like chair-canes ; crinoline, by some unfortunate woman who was afflicted by disjointed
hips ; skirts long in front, by some unhappy
woman who had monkey's feet. It is the
same with all things. The maxim of Bis-
marck,* "*La force prime le droit*" ("Might
is right"), was not enounced by the Chan-
cellor of the German Empire until he was
sure of being the strongest.

The peacock, whose atrocious voice is well
known, said that the nightingale prevented
peaceful people from sleeping ; and the
turkey who grinned at the peacock's exer-

tion in the poultry-yard, said he disgraced his model.

I have not said all on in-door dresses. I will divide them in two categories: low-necked and high-necked.

The skirts of these dresses should be cut after the same principle: a train more or less long, and short enough in front to show the feet. Women who shrink from showing their feet are invariably those whose feet are badly formed and ill-shod. Only in waist should in-door dresses differ among themselves. High-necked dresses, if cut perfectly, showing the form of the bust of a well-made woman, will satisfy the most fastidious observer. Low-necked, when they show the shoulders and the summit of the bust, leaving the arms full-length bare, be the waist cut square or heart-form on the collar-bone, will always command the approval of lovers of the beautiful.

The most important thing in the dress, is incontestably the woman who wears it. If her neck is straight, a little long, gracefully inclining in front, her shoulders firm and large, her collar showing a very little, her arms round, white, and tapering, her chest not too much projecting, her skin fair and velvety, her back slightly hollow between the shoulders by a line entering the vertebral column, she need not in my opinion trouble her head about her style of waist. Whatever dress she wears will attract far less attention than herself. This is in short the end which every intelligent dress-maker should attain. To make the dress show a woman to advantage, and at the same time not make her remarkable. A dress should be to a woman what a frame is to a portrait.

CHAPTER XIII.

STREET dresses, while showing the feet like in-door dresses, should never train behind. I do not say make them as short as those of a shepherdess. I say they should not sweep the street, nor mud, yet be long enough to give grace to the carriage, remain slightly touching the ground. Here I may say a few words on female form. Ladies of medium size are often charming, but tall ladies alone are graceful. Beauty with woman is a thing apart from height. I will add more, tall ladies alone can be well-dressed, and the reason is a simple one: a large woman can be graceful, walking, sitting, standing, or crossing a brook. In any position she may take, the movements of her body are harmonious. A little woman, on the contrary, always has an embarrassing air. The smallness of her form intimidates; her movements are brusque and jerky.

Then by all means a woman should be tall. I do not mean large; on the contrary, if she wants to be considered handsome and well-dressed, she should be tall.

The accessories that show to advantage a dress, are the many skirts. From principle, I object to an abuse of them; because they only serve to disguise the legs, stiffen the movements of a woman's carriage, and give her the air of a board advancing by the effect of some interior mechanism. A narrow skirt, besides having the advantage of revealing the movements and costing a great deal less, makes a woman appear tall and slight.

———————

CHAPTER XIV.

CORSETS, objects of the animadversion of Jean Jacques Rousseau, who attributed to them the greater part of all grave maladies of women, have survived the Genevan philosopher, and do not seem to disappear. Those that are made at the present day, with clasps in front, do not deform the waist nor the busts of women, as did those our great-grandmothers wore. They are convenient and elegant. It is true, though hidden from sight, they might possibly meet insolent observers and be possibly exposed to view, like garters. Then it is not a bad idea, nor is it an immoral one, to ornament, trim, and embroider them with pretty

edging, bows, ribbon, and lace ; also to make
them of silk, satin, etc. A woman who is
blessed with fair, pinkish skin, and mignon
blue veins, will find a black satin one very
becoming. The same of a lady with dull
skin ; that is to say, a yellow tint would not
regret wearing a crimson satin one.

It is indispensable to be a colorist when
one undertakes to please ; that is why one
must be a little artistic when they undertake
to dress a woman. I believe myself to be so,
and have made all studies necessary to become an artist. I hope I shall not die until I
have tried the dress-making trade. There is
a third accessory on which it is well to pon-
der. I refer to the article that shows to advantage the folds of the skirt and gives it a
sort of graceful regularity, that women call a
bustle, and dress-makers a polisson. This
indispensable article, I am told, and I would
wish to believe, is nothing less than the bustle
our great-great-grandmothers wore. I want to
show how the progress of ideas and revolu-
tions aid and change the well-being and utility of things. Bustle, in Spanish, was com-

posed of two words—Vertugado—virtue and
guard ; hence we see how things were trans-
formed and changed in the sixteenth century.
It was, says Madame de Mattville, a monstrous round machine, like several barrel-
hoops, forming a cylinder, and making the
waist quite slim. Some women wore a kind
of stuffed pad made of horse-hair, and even
whalebone in the upper part of their dresses,
enclosing all the trunk from the hips down.

Women, by passively submitting themselves to wear these ridiculous machines, did
not tarry long to make them objects of fashion
that gave grace to their costume.

The charter had good bills in those times !

CHAPTER XV.

I DO not believe it necessary to remark
that the fashion of paniers sprang
from hoop-skirts, and that crinoline
was the exaggerated result of paniers, be-

cause crinoline is simply the panier. prolonged. Gracious Heaven! exaggeration on exaggeration! but the women of the present day, have their bustles made of hair-cloth, and have reasonable ideas; still it often strikes me they are wanting in a little more when I think of the immense dimensions of their belt-bows, such knots placed as they are with flying streamers behind. To me they appear far from graceful, though they are not always without a motive. In the question of costumes, it is not sufficient that they are graceful and convenient; they should have also a really apparent utility. On this, perhaps, I am short-sighted, but I see no use for those bows placed on the waist. A silk sash of bright colors tied closely around the waist, such as I have seen Spanish ladies wear when riding horseback, has some charm about it. But an article only composed of an enormous rosette, and two streamers falling to the heels, however gracefully arranged, has nothing stylish or picturesque about it.

I hope I am understood. I do not wish to make unreasonable war against belt-bows. I find them about as well placed as they are graceful. The rules of plastic art are, that a woman, to be well-formed, should be tall, with a small, round, flexible waist, large hips and shoulders, and the upper part of her chest projecting a little, with her arms straight on each side, falling with easy grace from her bust.

All the different articles of female adjustment tend to show the form to advantage, and those mentioned here merit to be preserved. The rest should be cast aside.

I declare then in favor of the Spanish *sash*, or silk scarf, tied very tight around the waist, and I object to the enormous belt-bows behind.

CHAPTER XVI.

I WILL terminate this philippic *à propos* of belt-bows by disagreeing with Jean Jacques Rousseau—that tasteless Savoyard, who had nothing artistic in him, but who, it appears to me, followed too much his inclinations for the trivial and common in the campaign he took up against corsets and bodices. The thick, large, flat waists of Swiss dairy-maids may have had a charm for the Genevan philosopher, but to a man of taste they are simply hideous. It is incontestable that corsets have their danger, but only when badly made; many of them are like shoes made by ignorant shoemakers to protect the feet—they only deform and hurt them. Women should be strictly on their guard against the despotism of corset-makers. They should never accept from their hands instruments of torture that compromise the beauty of their form, as well as their health. Corsets were not

only made to show to advantage the exquisite beauties of the female form, but principally to sustain the waist and protect the
chest against shocks or blows. It is, then, essential that they should not press or in any
way hurt the organs which they are intended to protect. A well-made corset
should support the bosom in its normal
position, without crushing or pressing it ; and
should also keep the waist straight without impeding its flexibility, and render it
small without too tight lacing, which crowds
the organs one on the other. To be thus
made it should be far from stiffening the
waist, and never prevent the easy bending
of the body. It can only do this when it is
at the same time strong, supple, and flexible.
The whalebones that form the body of the
corset, and the busks, above all, should be
supple, carefully chosen, and frequently reno-
vated. A perfectly made corset is a rare
thing—more than rare, it is a miracle. The
woman who feels absolutely sure of the
beauty of her form would do well not to
wear any.

To return to the subject of dresses. Without specifying any absolute style on the form of them, which varies according to the season, climate, manners, politics, and customs of all people, I will say that of all forms of dress known, that which to me combines all the advantages of elegance, convenience, comfort, and ease, while covering the beauties of the female form, that can be worn without inconvenience in the street or house, in short, that can be made of the richest or simplest material,—is that which was worn by our great-great-grandmothers, and designated by dress-makers under the name of *Robe Watteau.*

CHAPTER XVII.

HERE take occasion to speak of winter and travelling garments, those that women wear to protect themselves against cold and humidity. Those gar-

ments are known by different names, such as
mantillas, cloaks, paletots, water-proofs, etc.,
etc., etc., varying each season according to
the caprices of fashion, but more frequently
the caprices of the dress-makers. There is
one garment that Parisian dress-makers have
not yet found, because it comes direct from
England and will erelong be all the rage in
the costume of women—I mean the water-
proof, that long flowing garment all in one
piece, that approaches as near antiquity as
the eternal long garment with immense plaits
that the Romans called *Pallium*, and Læna
and the Arabs called *Haik*, and which
seemed made expressly, in its primitive form,
to warm a man's body as long as he lived,
and to serve him for a shroud when dead.
The colored woollen robe, the only garment
worn by the Fellah women of modern
Egypt—they do not even wear chemises on
account of their poverty, without doubt—
seems to me to have been the model of the
water-proof. That garment without a belt, all
of one piece, falling around the body in drap-
ery and folds as they walk, open in three

12

parts—one to put their head through, and the other two for their arms, which remain completely bare up to the shoulder.

I must not forget to state, that in view of facilitating the backward and forward movements of the feet, the robe of the fellah is split open on one side only, from the armpit to the ankle ; a metal hook fastens the two folds of the stuff above the hip, and when the woman walks, her whole smooth body, like basalt, is nearly all exposed to view. The water-proof being a garment made to be specially worn over the dress, and to protect a woman from rain and cold, has not the same advantages or inconveniences as the garment of the Egyptian peasant. It does not expose a woman's person to public curiosity, yet it does not give the same freedom of movement to the body. Such as it is, however, the waterproof is perfectly adapted to our use. In damp weather, the umbrella only protects the head, never the shoulders ; while the water-proof protects the whole body. According to its thickness, it can also serve as a protection against extreme cold.

With sleeves and pockets it is a very useful garment, and when worn by a tall lady is not without grace. I have seen some very handsomely made at Gaildraud's. They were in blue cloth with *revers* of black velvet edged with white, and square silver-plated buttons. The great advantage of an over-garment like this is, it saves the wearer the trouble of dressing up to take a morning walk, ride in the cars, or go shopping on a dark day. A woman who has such a water-proof has no need of other than a colored skirt or little under-jacket. If she has good fitting shoes, as I hope she has, and her hair neatly dressed, she need not feel uneasy about her appearance or her costume. She is charming.

CHAPTER XVIII.

TRUST the pretty women who read this work will be convinced that I have not the slightest intention to dis- please them or to be absolutely disagreeable. If, however, I do not share the astonishing ideas of the fair sex—every one in this world has their weakness—I will not push the mania of costumes to such a point as to offend them. There is always some charita- ble reticence in the observations I address them. Nevertheless, this time, and by ex- ception, I humbly ask permission to express my thoughts, and nothing but my thoughts, on the grave question of *painting*.

If women, prompted by no other motive than that of pleasing men, paint their faces, I solemnly declare to them, in the name of the masculine sex, that they are going a false route and will only render themselves horrible. A light touch might be tolerated on a pale complexion : it serves wonderfully to show the brilliancy of the eyes, and lights up the face with a look of animation ; but a coating of white trashy powder, a common mixture of dangerous drugs, smeared from the neck to the roots of the hair, is simply repugnant, if not disgusting.

Each one's particular complexion depends on a host of causes that we are not permitted to abolish or transform—from our physical constitution, our temperament, from the diet we follow, the hygiene we practise, and the thickness of our epidermis, etc., etc., etc. Just as there are large and small men, blondes and brunettes, lymphatic and sanguine temperaments, fools and wise men, so there are complexions brown, white, red, muddy, yellow, green, olive, sallow, tanned, and pimpled. It is easily conceived then, that some one of those complexions, especially the poorest, belong uniquely to the morbid state of the constitution, and when persons wish to modify them, a physician should first be consulted. A woman who has a bilious, yellow, sallow complexion, should take good care of her liver. While that is affected, all the pomades she may put on her face will never whiten it. The same with those of a sunburnt or pimpled complexion; they should be immediately medically treated by using lotions and adjunctions, more particularly by laxatives and a severe diet. I do not allude to ringworm, which is treated by sulphur baths, etc., nor to any skin disease, as I am not a doctor and have no desire to become one. What I say is, skin diseases are invariably caused by some interior trouble, and for a woman who is anxious and careful for her beauty, there exists but one infallible remedy, and that is, to seek the aid of medical art.

Nature is much more intelligent herself than all the perfumers, hair-dressers, druggists, chemists, and manufacturers of cosmetics, and—question of health apart—gives invariably to each one of us the complexion we deserve to have. That is to say, the one that best harmonizes with our features, the color of our hair and eyes. With a great effort of imagination, I have at last understood that a human being could not be abso-

lutely satisfied with the face Nature had
given.   But this I cannot conceive, that a
creature, who has not even the slightest idea
of ameliorating her disposition, which might
perhaps be far easier done, has the absurd
pretension of changing her face.   All she
can do, the only end—even aided by science
and art, at the expense of intelligence, patience, and lots of money—obtained is, to
make herself uglier than ever.

CHAPTER XIX.

NE meets often, too often, in the public streets, unfortunate young women,
that simple-minded people might
think afflicted by some terrible disease, who,
in the eyes of sensible people, are simply
victims of some caprice of bad taste.

These women, these unfortunate ones, are
not, perhaps, extraordinarily beautiful, nor
are they ugly.   The greater part of them

might be called passably good-looking; a few of them might be called charming. Unfortunately, that does not satisfy their ambition. Nature has given them black, or brown, or blonde hair, complexions to match, youthful repose, eyes sufficiently làrge to see with, and even to "chain hearts." "In an hour of folly," they cut off their hair, and substitute for it an abominable yellow wig, paint their eyelids and lashes, soil their eyebrows with powdered charcoal, cover their face with flour, paint their lips and gums with red paste of a bad odor, and thus fearfully daubed, resembling the wax dolls one sees in toy-shops, they dare promenade in the sun, and brave the bright light of a theatre. And all this to please. They never imagine that they make people tremble. Will it be said that I am overdrawing the picture, and that this satire is strained? It is enough to take a promenade in the Bois de Boulogne or on the Champs Elysées, to be convinced of the contrary. Out of one hundred young women you meet, fifty are made up as I have

just described. I know not what ails female
youth, but seeing what they do, one would
believe they took an interest in the definite
triumph of ugliness. It must not be supposed that this spectacle, full of instruction,
given us by the women of the nineteenth
century, is absolutely unpublished. It is not
the first time that the world has seen such
prodigious efforts of ingenuity employed by
our companions, to destroy, one after another, all the beauties Heaven distributed
among them. Those of us who have sufficient knowledge to be able to lead our imagination back to Roman history and the
ancient society of Rome, can see a thousand
things superior to those that dazzle our eyes
in the present day.

There existed in Rome two temples dedicated to "Viril Fortune," a divinity who,
according to the belief of the Romans, had
power to hide from men the corporal defects
of women. One of these temples was near
the environs of the Porto Palatino, the other
at the Scelerate Gate. I know a few Parisian
ladies who, if Christianity had not violently

12*

put down all the divinities, even the most useful in paganism, would go regularly and pay their devotion to the temple of Viril Fortune. They might not be absolutely wrong in so doing.

But that is not the question. Then let it pass.

CHAPTER XX.

WHAT renders the Parisian ladies of the third Republic superior to the dames of the Roman Empire is, the latter were simply ridiculous enough to seek means to remedy the inevitable ravages of Nature, by only using cosmetics when they were old and decrepit, while the French ladies have not the patience and the courage to wait so long, but in their youth of bloom and beauty they seek to embellish themselves at the cost of spoiling their charms. A Roman lady of the upper class, in the time of Cæsar, or even Titus, always had a special room in her house, where slaves proceeded to care for her toilette and the restoration of her charms. This room, among the wealthy class, was generally spacious and adorned with mirrors, and very handsome polished metal frames, and around the room were several wardrobes filled with the different clothing and ornaments that served to adorn the mistress of the house.

The women of the present day imagine they are doing something quite new in choosing for hair-dye yellow and carrot color. They also think it a proof of originality to wear false hair.

A contemporary matron of Caligula, if she returned to this world, would pity them. As it was fashionable in the Roman Empire to do everything great, a respectable woman, who wished to please, invariably made her *début* in society by shaving off all her hair. It was an Egyptian custom with the women of Thebes and Memphis, in the time of Rhamses IV.—Sesostris—and adopted to keep the brain clear.

Nature having given them all a great quan-

tity of fine black hair, they found it annoy-
ing and uncomfortable, so they shaved it off
so close that their heads were as smooth as
their knees.　They then delicately placed a
pretty little wig of silk floss, powdered with
blue or gold dust, which they considered in-
finitely more gracious and light.　It was in
this apparel, with her eyes painted and her
body decked, that the celebrated Cleopatra
appeared when she made the road to the
hearts of so many illustrious men in her time,
Cæsar among them.

But to return to the Roman dames.　Just
as to-day an elegant woman, *chic* as they say
at Versailles, has in her wardrobe apparel of
all sorts and colors, appropriate for each season of the year, so a matron in the good
days of the Empire had in hers all kinds
of wigs varying in color.　Hair, during
the reign of Claudius, formed a great article
of commerce.　The red came from Germany, the black from Egypt, the brown from
Gaul, and the blonde from Greece.　But it is
evident that it was not enough for a woman,
anxious to please, rejuvenate and embellish

herself, to apply like a cap a wig all dressed with braids mixed with precious stones, on her shaved head.

When the choice of a wig * was made, it was necessary to arrange the eyebrows, eyelashes, and complexion of the person who wore it, in harmony with its color.

It was then that slaves were specially charged with the make-up of the face, which they did to their heart's content. It would require several pages to copy the names of all the pomades, pastes, ointments, and cosmetics which were enclosed in alabaster and tin jars, that served for the delicate operation which Cicero called "*Medicamenta candoris et ruboris.*"

All I can say is, they were composed principly of crocodile muck, that passed for whitening the skin, but had the disagreeable advantage of melting when exposed to the sun, which made them prefer chalk diluted with the aid of acid.

---

* The wigs, when all mounted, were named galeria. See Juvenal, p. 120, v. 6.

This latter paste admirably resisted the sun, but could not resist the rain.

CHAPTER XXI.

WE are led to hope that erelong the Parisian ladies will imitate the Roman, by the plurality of wigs. For my part, I think it the surest and most expedient means to place them on a level with the love of change that is innate with all mankind. Imagine a husband possessing a wife of various colors ; he would never have the slightest occasion to be untrue to her. His fancy to that end would be without excuse. When the desire to change "colors" took possession of him, all he had to do to satisfy himself would be to ask his wife to change her wig.

A question that threatens to become almost as serious and interesting as that of crinoline, is the one about bonnets. Let us be of good faith. Crinoline, with its inevitable iron cage, had not force enough to battle against the narrow dresses; so bonnets, with their ugly forms hiding the hair, cannot long hold out against their rivals, round hats. The round hat—that till the present day, was only worn in the country, travelling, and at the seaside ; which in its picturesque form can be varied to the extreme, shows the nape of the neck, and lends itself to all kinds of trimming, flowers, feathers, laces ; in short, show a child's face as well as a woman's to advantage—becomes a brunette as well as a blonde.

What pleases me in a round hat, and why I take sides with it as I did with narrow dresses, is because it is preferable to a bonnet, and becomes almost all physiognomies. Every woman in the least pretty need not wait the decision of her milliner, or the opinion of the venerable Viscountess de Renneville, but can vary the form, material, and trimming to suit herself.

Time was when bonnets triumphed, when at any place of public amusement women invariably looked as if dressed alike, and appeared all in one style. To-day, it is the contrary; each woman has her own style of hair-dressing, and wears the hat she pleases, as the reflection of her own taste and liking. And it is no small task to be able to harmonize the form of the hat with the features Nature has given.

All women, thank God, have not noses alike, nor foreheads, nor chins, nor even cheeks. There are some, though, whose united features remind one in the distance of the type so characteristic and well known under the name of "Punchinello;" others appear like young swells, on account of their exuberance and health. Everybody is aware that the same system of hair-dressing or the same hat is not becoming to physiognomies so unlike. But I will let caricatures end, and return to the subject of beauty.

The despotism of manufacturers of millinery goods has till now been too long tolerated; now it is time that women who, by their education, natural disposition, and in-

nate taste, are more competent to eate
fashions than any one else, should take turns
each one in the movement and direction of
fashion. If public taste grows false day by
day, if the ugly and the false predominate
in everything, it does not spring from any
deviation or weakness from the beautiful in
our country. France, thank God, has not
been conquered, and she never will be on
the soil of art, taste, and sentiment for the
beautiful. The only thing that in part coun-
terbalances her artistic and intellectual
superiority, is the respect of routine. We
hardly dare to innovate, in the puerile fear of
ceasing to resemble "*tout le monde.*" Simi-
liarity makes the law in questions of fashion
and those illustrated fashion papers which
especially treat, in God knows what language,
the most delicate matters that concern ladies'
toilettes, doing all they can with the object
of advertising the worship of the common in
defiance of the beautiful.

CHAPTER XXII.

THE question of hats would be incomplete, if the mention of artificial flowers were omitted. In view of that, I hasten to make known to my readers a discovery I recently made.

I will begin by an anecdote:

I am fortunate enough to reside in the house with an adorable little girl five years of age, whose black eyes, blonde hair, and goodness of heart would turn any man's head. Every day when the weather is fine she goes to promenade in the Park, the Museum, or the *Bois de Boulogne*, with her nurse or her mother; and as she is passionately fond of flowers, she rarely returns without bringing an immense bouquet.

Thus have I seen, day by day, the spring-time in the vases that adorn the mantel in my library; sometimes violets, lilacs, marigolds, and daisies.

Fifteen days since, entering my library

I found my little girl seated before a table, her doll on her knee, and picking over a mass of daisies, rose-buds, and other flowers.

I took a few in my hand; they seemed dying. "You should hasten and put them in water, my pet," said I to her; "they are fading."

The little rogue began to laugh. "Oh, how silly papa is!" said she to her mother. "He thought these flowers came from the Bois de Boulogne; it was Madame Peyrut who made them and gave them to me this morning."

Remember well, my readers, that at the age of sixteen I was a first-class botanist, and I never would admit that there was a possibility of my mistaking an artificial flower for a natural one.

The only excuse I can frame to explain such a deception was the wonderful perfection of the flowers I held in my hand, and of which I mechanically smelled as if they exhaled some odor, each one was so flexibly placed on its stem, its petals turned one on the other with such a truthful appearance. In fact, there was such perfection in their softness, simplicity, and lifelikeness one would almost wish to eat them.

CHAPTER XXIII.

HIS little adventure so occupied me, that for several days I wanted to know Madame Peyrut, with no other view than to compliment her on her talent. It was enough for me to exchange a few words with her to be convinced that she was a true artist. While talking, she showed me her collection of flowers, and indeed it was a collection in every sense of the word. There was enough to occupy the leisure moments of a lover of Nature, which I flatter myself to be, and a hundred women of good taste, as well as all admirers of the beautiful.

Bunches of currants, clusters of grapes, red and white, with such a look of acidity and freshness as to make one's teeth water;

bunches of cherries, capable of attracting
blackbirds ; pansies of so fresh a color, they
surpassed the natural ones. I remember particularly among them a certain water-lily,
large, open, with its long, undulating stem,
which was beautiful beyond imagination. I
have said Madame Peyrut was a veritable artist. If she had not been a florist she should
have been a painter. The first thing she observed in her garden walks was that the Lord's
flowers bore no resemblance to those of a
florist, which were generally straight as if
their stems were sustained by threads of iron.
Another thing that she discovered was, that
each shrub had a certain pose, and combina-
tion of particular colors ; in short, a really
picturesque, decided type of its own. Thus
the brier, condemned to all eternity to pro-
ject its long, thorny branches in the sun-
light on the woodside, has a fertility about
it, even though its leaves are covered with
dust.   It differs from the water-lily destined
to float on the surface of the water, with its
spreading leaves and long, tough stem rooted
in the river's mud. Even the daisy has

not the same form as the ranunculus, nor does the marsh mallow grow like the fox-glove, any more than the lily grows like the poppy. One might name an infinite number of comparisons.

The real talent consists in seizing the colors and imitating them as nearly as possible to the real. All flowers that have been seen, up to the present day, from the hands of florists, falsely represented as having a well-earned reputation, have had invariably a dry look about them, that made them appear and smell more like a made flower than a field one. They were awkwardly straight on their wires, with no look of freshness about them, their petals and filaments hard and stiff, in fact nothing delusive about them. But with Madame Peyrut, thanks to the simplest means, a rich pallet of colors, a little brush, little branches of paper, fine bits of light muslin, a little pot of gum, imperceptible rubber tubes, the whole worked, it is true, by fairy fingers' and able hands of the workwomen, these flowers obtained their poetic grace, charming colors and freshness from the sap and light. The artist left nothing undone to render them natural and life-like. The leaves lightly rolled one on the other, their edges slightly faded as if burned by the sun, little grains of dust, drops of dew, little insects lighted on them as if in a garden. The most natural beauties Nature gave to plants were here, and all they needed to be original was perfume.

What seems most singular in the making of artificial flowers is, that every workwoman has her specialty for making a certain flower, fruit, or vine, and thus spends all her time doing some little labor attached to it, knowing nothing but this special branch of her trade, being even incapable of becoming interested in what her neighbor is operating. Thus one makes the tendrils of certain flowers, another the vines, another the stems, another the petals, and a fourth the cholacis. But the true artist herself directs, invents, and re-unites all the scattered material, and the slightest object passing through her hands in an elementary state, when laid aside, has all the appearance and charm of life.

CHAPTER XXIV.

RTIFICIAL flowers alone do not constitute a lady's head-dress. They are simply graceful, poetic ornaments, nothing more. It is quite an art to pose them gracefully on a hat.

A woman of taste and intelligence should not call on any one to trim her hat, any more than to trim her feet, her hands, or her hair. She can buy the forms at the manufacturer's, and find at her pleasure silk, velvet, plumes, ribbons, flowers, and lace.

It is truly astonishing the elegance of some ladies' hats. The prettiest are generally those that have been made up, trimmed, thrown aside, and perhaps retrimmed a hundred times, before they were finished by the wearers. But it is now time to treat the question of veils.

Veils are naturally in two great categories: those that are destined to hide the face, and those that are destined to show it to advantage.

The first are only worn by old, homely, wrinkled women, afflicted with some skin disease, or by women who have some reason to conceal their face. Under such circumstances, they are necessarily never too thick nor too heavy ; therefore, I will not discuss them.

The second are necessary to complete the dress of every pretty young woman.

Destined to preserve the complexion from the strong rays of the sun, and at the same time to give a smooth, mysterious softness to the skin, they are never too thin under such circumstances.

The most elegant and irresistible, when worn by a brunette with beautiful black eyes, are the large white tulle called *illusion tulle.* I know of none so fascinating and jaunty as those veils. They cover the hat and face, and are fastened in the back or under the chin in a bow, and the charm they give the face is ideal.

13

CHAPTER XXV.

DO not condemn the little veils that are worn on hats and come down to the nose, resembling a light, transparent mask. If I prefer the large ones, it is because I think them more poetic; especially when blown by the wind, if they reveal a pair of large black eyes. This need not depreciate in the least the small ones. The merit depends very much on the beauty of the person who wears them.

Blondes, brunettes, and ladies who are born with red hair, have the bad taste to wear yellow chignons, and for this reason I would recommend them not to wear green or light-brown veils. They are not becoming; black, white, and blue are the only ones becoming to blondes.

Fat, plump, puffy women, with thick waists and immense hips, would do well not to wear those little jockey sailor hats with imperceptible rims, that certain milliners have the mania of posing on everybody's head. Those hats should be left to slim people. These same majestics would do better still never to use their heads as dessert-plates, by emptying the contents of a basket of cherries on them.

I am very fond of this beautiful fruit, particularly when I see it somewhere else than on dyed or undyed hair on women of weight. I could add as much on prunes, apricots, even peaches, and sometimes small pumpkins.

Now, like a threaded needle, line by line following the precept of La Bruyère, I have studied women from head to foot, directing her by good counsels and watchful criticisms, I think I may crown the work by making some comments on perfumes.

CHAPTER XXVI.

ERFUMES are to women what dew is to the flowers, song to the birds, stars to the sky ; a sort of indispensable complement, one might almost say seasoning. A young, pretty, well-dressed woman, when at the promenade, if she wishes to be completely fascinating, should leave on her tracks a particularly exquisite, attractive odor.

The great difficulty with women desirous to please is, to know the perfumes best suited to their style of beauty, without injury to their health. At the risk of passing for a fantastic mind, I will offer two propositions that contain a germ entirely theoretical on the use of perfumes for the female toilet.

One thing a woman—if she is young, handsome, intelligent, and elegant, possessing good qualities of the body, heart, and mind, as my lady readers must necessarily have—should do, is, never seek to resemble a flower, be it ever so fragrant, because it has but one perfume ; but she may seek to resemble a bouquet, whose principal charm consists in the union of numerous exquisite odors. The woman who does this will have a particular perfume for each part of her person.

The second proposition differs slightly from the first. It is the result of a profound conviction with me. Like certain colors that seen made expressly to mingle with the beauty of certain women, so a particular type of beauty requires a particular kind of perfume. The perfume that suits a brunette would not suit a blonde.

No one can trace a reasonable rule on this subject. It is one of those things that cannot be analyzed, but is felt. It is then the duty of each woman to use the perfume that is best suited to her particular style of beauty.

Here are a few general remarks to terminate : 1st. Perfumes should be light, penetrating, and always resemble one of the odors of flowers. 2d. Musk and patchouly should be avoided as a, pest. 3d. Eau de

Cologne is only fit for porters and Germans. 4th. Arabian jessamine, heliotrope, pink, and rose seem expressly intended for large women with black hair, dull skin, red lips, and fiery glances.

Strawberry, lily of the valley, and vervain will be judiciously employed by blondes with golden locks and dark blue eyes.

Nothing for yellow chignons.

PARIS, *Oct.*, 1872.

THE END.

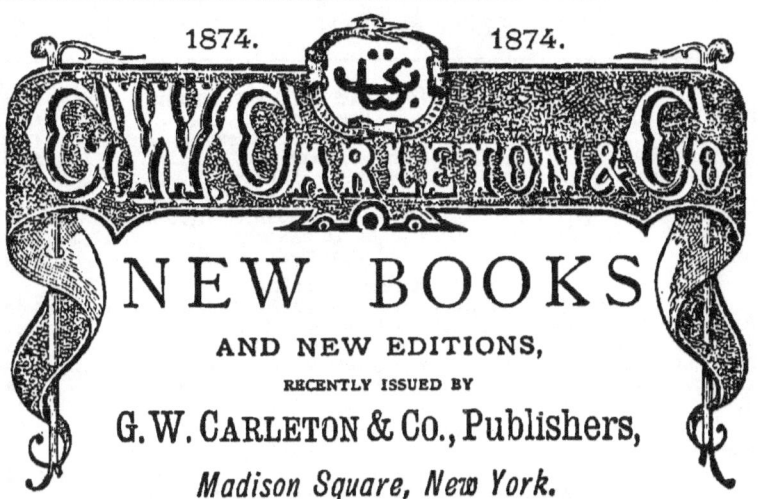

1874. 1874.

NEW BOOKS

AND NEW EDITIONS,

RECENTLY ISSUED BY

G. W. CARLETON & Co., Publishers,

Madison Square, New York.

The Publishers, upon receipt of the price in advance, will send any book on this Catalogue by mail, *postage free*, to any part of the United States.

All books in this list [unless otherwise specified] are handsomely bound in cloth board binding, with gilt backs, suitable for libraries.

Mary J. Holmes' Works.

TEMPEST AND SUNSHINE..........$1 50	DARKNESS AND DAYLIGHT.........$1 50
ENGLISH ORPHANS................... 1 50	HUGH WORTHINGTON.............. 1 50
HOMESTEAD ON THE HILLSIDE...... 1 50	CAMERON PRIDE 1 50
'LENA RIVERS...................... 1 50	ROSE MATHER..................... 1 50
MEADOW BROOK..................... 1 50	ETHELYN'S MISTAKE.............. 1 50
DORA DEANE....................... 1 50	MILLBANK........................ 1 50
COUSIN MAUDE..................... 1 50	EDNA BROWNING......(new)....... 1 50
MARIAN GRAY...................... 1 50	

Marion Harland's Works.

ALONE............................$1 50	SUNNYBANK $1 50
HIDDEN PATH...................... 1 50	HUSBANDS AND HOMES............ 1 50
MOSS SIDE........................ 1 50	RUBY'S HUSBAND 1 50
NEMESIS.......................... 1 50	PHEMIE'S TEMPTATION........... 1 50
MIRIAM........................... 1 50	THE EMPTY HEART................ 1 50
AT LAST.......................... 1 50	TRUE AS STEEL......(new) 1 50
HELEN GARDNER.................... 1 50	JESSAMINE....(just published).... 1 50

Charles Dickens' Works.
"*Carleton's New Illustrated Edition.*"

THE PICKWICK PAPERS.............$1 50	MARTIN CHUZZLEWIT.............$1 50
OLIVER TWIST..................... 1 50	OUR MUTUAL FRIEND 1 50
DAVID COPPERFIELD............... 1 50	TALE OF TWO CITIES 1 50
GREAT EXPECTATIONS............. 1 50	CHRISTMAS BOOKS................ 1 50
DOMBEY AND SON.................. 1 50	SKETCHES BY "BOZ". 1 50
BARNABY RUDGE................... 1 50	HARD TIMES, etc................. 1 50
NICHOLAS NICKLEBY............... 1 50	PICTURES OF ITALY, etc......... 1 50
OLD CURIOSITY SHOP............. 1 50	UNCOMMERCIAL TRAVELLER........ 1 50
BLEAK HOUSE...................... 1 50	EDWIN DROOD, etc................ 1 50
LITTLE DORRIT.................... 1 50	MISCELLANIES 1 50

Augusta J. Evans' Novels.

BEULAH..........................$1 75	ST. ELMO........................ 1 75
MACARIA.......................... 1 75	VASHTI......(new)............... 1 75
INEZ............................. 1 75	

Captain Mayne Reid—Illustrated.

SCALP HUNTERS	$1 50	WHITE CHIEF	$1 50
WAR TRAIL	1 50	HEADLESS HORSEMAN	1 50
HUNTER'S FEAST	1 50	LOST LENORE	1 50
TIGER HUNTER	1 50	WOOD RANGERS	1 50
OSCEOLA, THE SEMINOLE	1 50	WILD HUNTRESS	1 50
THE QUADROON	1 50	THE MAROON	1 50
RANGERS AND REGULATORS	1 50	RIFLE RANGERS	1 50
WHITE GAUNTLET	1 50	WILD LIFE	1 50

A. S. Roe's Works.

A LONG LOOK AHEAD	$1 50	TRUE TO THE LAST	$1 50
TO LOVE AND TO BE LOVED	1 50	LIKE AND UNLIKE	1 50
TIME AND TIDE	1 50	LOOKING AROUND	1 50
I'VE BEEN THINKING	1 50	WOMAN OUR ANGEL	1 50
THE STAR AND THE CLOUD	1 50	THE CLOUD ON THE HEART	1 50
HOW COULD HE HELP IT	1 50	RESOLUTION (new)	1 50

Hand-Books of Society.

THE HABITS OF GOOD SOCIETY. The nice points of taste and good manners, and the art of making oneself agreeable........$1 75

THE ART OF CONVERSATION.—A sensible work, for every one who wishes to be either an agreeable talker or listener........1 50

THE ARTS OF WRITING, READING, AND SPEAKING.—An excellent book for self-instruction and improvement........1 50

A NEW DIAMOND EDITION of the above three popular books.—Small size, elegantly bound, and put in a box........3 00

Mrs. Hill's Cook Book.

MRS. A. P. HILL'S NEW COOKERY BOOK, and family domestic receipts........$2 00

Charlotte Bronte and Miss Muloch.

SHIRLEY.—Author of Jane Eyre...$1 75 | JOHN HALIFAX, GENTLEMAN......$1 75

Mrs. N. S. Emerson.

BETSEY AND I ARE OUT—And other Poems. A Thanksgiving Story........$1 50

Louisa M. Alcott.

MORNING GLORIES—A beautiful juvenile, by the author of "Little Women".....1 50

The Crusoe Books—Famous "Star Edition."

ROBINSON CRUSOE.—New illustrated edition			$1 50
SWISS FAMILY ROBINSON.	Do.	Do	1 50
THE ARABIAN NIGHTS.	Do.	Do	1 50

Julie P. Smith's Novels.

WIDOW GOLDSMITH'S DAUGHTER	$1 75	THE WIDOWER	$1 75
CHRIS AND OTHO	1 75	THE MARRIED BELLE	1 75
TEN OLD MAIDS [in press]	1 75		

Artemus Ward's Comic Works.

ARTEMUS WARD—HIS BOOK	$1 50	ARTEMUS WARD—IN LONDON	$1 50
ARTEMUS WARD—HIS TRAVELS	1 50	ARTEMUS WARD—HIS PANORAMA	1 50

Fanny Fern's Works.

FOLLY AS IT FLIES	$1 50	CAPER-SAUCE (new)	$1 50
GINGERSNAPS	1 50	A MEMORIAL.—By JAMES Parton	2 00

Josh Billings' Comic Works.

JOSH BILLINGS' PROVERBS	$1 50	JOSH BILLINGS FARMER'S ALMINAX, 25 cts.	
JOSH BILLINGS ON ICE	1 50	(In paper covers.)	

Verdant Green.

A racy English college story—with numerous comic illustrations........$1 50

Popular Italian Novels.

DOCTOR ANTONIO.—A love story of Italy. By Ruffini........$1 75
BEATRICE CENCI.—By Guerrazzi. With a steel Portrait........1 75

M. Michelet's Remarkable Works.

LOVE (L'AMOUR).—English translation from the original French			$1 50
WOMAN (LA FEMME).	Do.	Do.	Do.	1 50

Ernest Renan's French Works.

THE LIFE OF JESUS $1 75	LIFE OF SAINT PAUL.............$1 75
LIVES OF THE APOSTLES 1 75	BIBLE IN INDIA. By Jacolliot.... 2 00

Geo. W. Carleton.

OUR ARTIST IN CUBA.—With 50 comic illustrations of life and customs...... .$1 50
OUR ARTIST IN PERU.   Do.   Do.   Do, ... 1 50
OUR ARTIST IN AFRICA. (In press)   Do.   Do. 1 50

May Agnes Fleming's Novels.

GUY EARLESCOURT'S WIFE.........$1 75 | A WONDERFUL WOMAN. $1 75

Maria J. Westmoreland's Novels.

HEART HUNGRY.................$1 75 | CLIFFORD TROUP   (new)......$1 75

Sallie A. Brock's Novels.

KENNETH, MY KING...............$1 75 | A NEW BOOK......(in press)......

Don Quixote.

A BEAUTIFUL NEW 12MO EDITION. With illustrations by Gustave Dore........$1 50

Victor Hugo.

LES MISERABLES.—English translation from the French. Octavo............$2 50
LES MISERABLES.—In the Spanish language............................ ...... 5 00

Algernon Charles Swinburne.

LAUS VENERIS, AND OTHER POEMS.—An elegant new edition...... ....$1 50
FRENCH LOVE-SONGS.—Selected from the best French authors....... .... 1 50

Robert Dale Owen.

THE DEBATABLE LAND... ....$2 00 | THREADING MY WAY—Autobiography$1 50

Guide for New York City.

WOOD'S ILLUSTRATED HAND-BOOK.—A beautiful pocket volume...............$1 00

The Game of Whist.

POLE ON WHIST.—The late English standard work............................$1 00

Mansfield T. Walworth's Novels.

WARWICK......................$1 75	STORMCLIFF $1 75
LULU....................... ... 1 75	DELAPLAINE......................... 1 75
HOTSPUR 1 75	BEVERLY...... (new)..............·· 1 75
A NEW NOVEL......(in press)......	

Mother Goose Set to Music.

MOTHER GOOSE MELODIES.—With music for singing, and illustrations $1 50

Tales from the Operas.

THE PLOTS OF POPULAR OPERAS in the form of stories............ ....$1 50

M. M. Pomeroy "Brick."

SENSE—(a serious book).........$1 50	NONSENSE—(a comic book) $1 50
GOLD-DUST do. 1 50	BRICK-DUST do. 1 50
OUR SATURDAY NIGHTS ... 1 50	LIFE OF M. M POMEROY........ ... 1 50

John Esten Cooke's Works.

FAIRFAX.........................$1 50	HAMMER AND RAPIER.............$1 50
HILT TO HILT.................... 1 50	OUT OF THE FOAM................. 1 50
A NEW BOOK......(in press).......	

Joseph Rodman Drake.

THE CULPRIT FAY.—The well-known faery poem, with 100 illustrations........$2 00
THE CULPRIT FAY.   Do.   superbly bound in turkey morocco.. 5 00

Richard B. Kimball's Works.

WAS HE SUCCESSFUL?.........$1 75	LIFE IN SAN DOMINGO.........$1 50
UNDERCURRENTS OF WALL STREET. 1 75	HENRY POWERS, BANKER 1 75
SAINT LEGER 1 75	TO-DAY............................ 1 75
ROMANCE OF STUDENT LIFE....... . 1 75	EMILIE......(in press)...........

Author "New Gospel of Peace."

CHRONICLES OF GOTHAM.—A rich modern satire (paper covers) ....25 cts.
THE FALL OF MAN.—A satire on the Darwin theory do.   ....50 cts.

Celia E. Gardner's Novels.

STOLEN WATERS.................$1 50 | BROKEN DREAMS,.................$1 50

Olive Logan.
WOMEN AND THEATRES.—And other miscellaneous topics.....................$1 50

Anna Cora Mowatt.
ITALIAN LIFE AND LEGENDS ......$1 50 | THE CLERGYMAN'S WIFE.—A novel.$1 75

Dr. Cummings's Works.

THE GREAT TRIBULATION.........$2 00	THE GREAT CONSUMMATION.......$2 00
THE GREAT PREPARATION..........2 00	THE SEVENTH VIAL.................2 00

Cecelia Cleveland.
THE STORY OF A SUMMER ; OR, JOURNAL LEAVES FROM CHAPPAQUA............$1 50

Dr. A. Cazenave.
THE ART OF HUMAN DECORATION. Translated from the French $1 50

Samuel Wilberforce.
LITTLE WANDERERS. Sunday Stories for Children. Illustrated.............$1 50

" Bill Arp."
PEACE PAPERS.—And other sketches. With comic illustrations................$1 50

Miscellaneous Works.

BRAZEN GATES.—A juvenile $1 50	CHRISTMAS HOLLY.-Marion Harland$1 50
ANTIDOTE TO GATES AJAR....... 25 cts	DREAM MUSIC.—F. R. Marvin..... 1 50
THE RUSSIAN BALL (paper)....... 25 cts	POEMS.—By L. G. Thomas........ 1 50
THE SNOBLACE BALL do ..... 25 cts	VICTOR HUGO.—His life........... 2 00
DEAFNESS.—Dr. E. B. Lighthill... 1 00	BEAUTY IS POWER 1 50
A BOOK ABOUT LAWYERS.......... 2 00	WOMAN, LOVE, AND MARRIAGE.... 1 50
A BOOK ABOUT DOCTORS.......... 2 00	WICKEDEST WOMAN in New York. 25 cts
SQUIBOB PAPERS.—John Phœnix... 1 50	SANDWICHES.—By Artemus Ward.. 25 cts
WIDOW SPRIGGINS.—Widow Bedott. 1 75	REGINA.—Poems by Eliza Cruger.. 1 50

Plymouth Church,—Brooklyn.
HISTORY OF THIS CHURCH ; from 1847 to 1873.—Portraits and illustration.....$2 00

Miscellaneous Novels.

LOYAL UNTO DEATH........ .. ..$1 75	BOBERT GREATHOUSE.—J. F. Swift. 2 00
BESSIE WILMERTON.—Westcott..... 1 50	FAUSTINA.—From the German..... 1 50
PURPLE AND FINE LINEN.—Fawcett. 1 75	MAURICE.—From the French....... 1 50
EDMUND DAWN.—By Ravenswood. 1 50	GUSTAVE ADOLF.—From the Swedish 1 50
CACHET.—Mrs. M. J. R. Hamilton. 1 50	ADRIFT WITH A VENGEANCE...... 1 50
THE BISHOP'S SON.—Alice Cary.... 1 75	UP BROADWAY.—By Eleanor Kirk.. 1 50
MARK GILDERSLEEVE.-J.S.Sauzade 1 75	MONTALBAN....................... 1 75
FERNANDO DE LEMOS.—C. Gayaree 2 00	LIFE AND DEATH................. 1 50
CROWN JEWELS.—Mrs. Moffat...... 1 75	CLAUDE GUEUX.—By Victor Hugo. 1 50
A LOST LIFE.—By Emily Moore.... 1 50	FOUR OAKS.—By Kamba Thorpe... 1 75
AVERY GLIBUN.—Orpheus C. Kerr. 2 00	ADRIFT IN DIXIE.—Edmund Kirke. 1 50
THE CLOVEN FOOT.— Do. . 1 50	AMONG THE GUERILLAS. Do. . 1 50
O. C. KERR PAPERS.—4 vols. in 1 . 2 00	AMONG THE PINES. Do. . 1 50
ROMANCE OF RAILROAD.—Smith... 1 50	MY SOUTHERN FRIENDS. Do. . 1 50
GENESIS DISCLOSED.—T.A. Davies. 1 50	DOWN IN TENNESSEE. Do. . 1 50

Miscellaneous Works.
A BOOK OF EPITAPHS.—Amusing, quaint, and curious......(new) $1 50
SOUVENIRS OF TRAVEL.—By Madame Octavia Walton LeVert................. 2 00
THE ART OF AMUSING.—A book of home amusements, with illustrations 1 50
HOW TO MAKE MONEY ; and how to keep it.—By Thomas A. Davies.......... 1 50
BALLAD OF LORD BATEMAN.—With Illustrations by Cruikshank (paper)... ...25 cts
BEHIND THE SCENES ; at the "White House."—By Elizabeth Keckley...... 2 00
THE YACHTMAN'S PRIMER.—For amateur sailors. T. R. Warren (paper).....50 cts
RURAL ARCHITECTURE.—By M. Field. With plans and illustrations.......... 2 00
LIFE OF HORACE GREELEY.—By L. U. Reavis. With a new steel Portrait.... 2 00
WHAT I KNOW OF FARMING.—By Horace Greeley............................ 1 50
PRACTICAL TREATISE ON LABOR.—By Hendrick B. Wright.................. 2 00
TWELVE VIEWS OF HEAVEN.—By Twelve Distinguished English Divines...:... 1 50
HOUSES NOT MADE WITH HANDS.—An illustrated juvenile, illust'd by Hoppin.. 1 00
CRUISE OF THE SHENANDOAH—The Last Confederate Steamer............... 1 50
MILITARY RECORD OF CIVILIAN APPOINTMENTS in the U. S. Army............ 5 00
IMPENDING CRISIS OF THE SOUTH.—By Hinton Rowan Helper............... 2 00
NEGROES IN NEGROLAND. Do. Do. Do. (paper covers). 1 00

* 9 7 8 3 3 3 7 3 7 0 7 6 3 *